FLESH & BLOOD

FLESH & BLOOD

Michèle Roberts

Published by VIRAGO PRESS Limited September 1994
42–43 Gloucester Crescent, Camden Town, London NW1 7PD

A CIP catalogue record for this title
is available from the British Library

Typeset by M Rules
Printed in Great Britain by
Mackays of Chatham plc

Acknowledgements

Thanks to Giuliana Schiavi for finding out for me about seventeenth-century Veneto names. Apologies to the inhabitants of the Veneto for inventing a new province and towns therein. Santa Salome *et al.* exist only in my imagination, their inhabitants likewise. Thanks to Anne McDermid of Curtis Brown, and to all at Virago, particularly Lennie Goodings and Fiona McIntosh, for their hard work and support. Thanks to all my friends and family. Special thanks to Jim Latter.

For Lily and Larry

FRED

An hour after murdering my mother I was in Soho. That was where it began. In the dress shop in Greek Street. In the changing room. I was on the run. A criminal. I saw myself: one of those men, framed in black, on a police poster; hollow-eyed, wild-haired, staring. I slowed my pace, tried to stop shaking. Tried to make myself invisible: dug my hands into my jacket pockets and slouched, my cap pulled low and my eyes swivelling from side to side to spot any approaching trouble.

I'd always had a gift for inventing stories. I shuffled them like a pack of cards in my head. When I made them up I believed they were true. Other people called them lies or excuses. I wondered what story to tell when I was caught, hauled to the cells. I couldn't imagine a story that would explain away my guilt. I was a killer. That was a fact.

In half an hour's time I was due to meet Martin outside the cinema in Wardour Street. This would be our third viewing of *Pierrot le Fou*. If Pierrot had to confess to murdering his mother he wouldn't care. I pictured thick lips pursed around a Gauloise, blue eyes frowning as the big mouth chewed, the skinny vest laying bare the broad shoulders. I lacked Belmondo's cool.

1

After the film Martin and I would go to a coffee-bar and talk. I'd try to tell him about the blood. I might ask him to help me to decide what to do.

I loafed along Old Compton Street to spin away the time. I prowled in and out of Italian grocery shops, checked the pyramids of strawberry tarts in the patisserie windows, surveyed the other strollers – the ones like myself who just looked, and the ones who preened, who offered themselves to my furtive gaze. A woman in silver brocade and stilettos. A girl in white plastic boots, white plastic mini-dress with cut-out holes. A slender boy, hair greased and quiffed, in drainpipes and brothel creepers. An old woman in a jade-green turban and a blue catsuit.

It began to rain. Fierce pellets of water hit the back of my neck and dripped inside my collar. I quickened my pace. To guilt I added chill misery. My jacket was no protection against the suddenly cool air, the wind which had sprung up. Raindrops slid down my eyelids and nose. I ducked around the street corner and into the nearest doorway, shivering.

Across the street glinted scrolls of coloured neon, scarlet and blue, that signalled cafés and restaurants. *Chez Mathilde. Benny's Jive Bar. L'Escargot.* The smell of food reached me through exhaust fumes and wet dust: fried onions and meat, roasting coffee, hot bread. Lunch-time; but I wasn't hungry. I took off my wet cap and squeezed it out, shook my head and let fly a scatter of water. My trouser legs clung damply to me, sent up the smell of wet wool. My feet squelched in my heavy shoes. I swore gently to myself and leaned back, further in, away from the rain.

Something cold and nubbly met my cheek. I twisted round, looked at the frosted glass panel of the door, varnished a sticky brown, that I was pressed against. A sprawl of gold script, blurring with rain. I made out *Madame Lesley. Modiste. Dress-Hire. Alterations.* The shop window, bellying out next to me, was blanked out by grey canvas blinds. I tried the door-handle, an S-shape in twisted brass, expecting it not to budge. But it turned easily, and let me inside.

Absence of rain and daylight. Warmth, scented with cinnamon and carnation. Like the inside of my mother's wardrobe, when I used to creep in there on wet days like this one and play with her things. A tunnel at the

2

back of her room, tight with frocks and suits on padded hangers ruched with silk. Apricot-coloured hangers, banana, salmon, hyacinth.

I'd lie on the floor and look upwards at the press of frocks. Sometimes I'd stretch up, slide my hands in between those soft drops of material, a finger-language I learned in silence, among lavender sachets, coiled narrow belts with gold buckles, racks of high-heeled shoes. Layers of smells: the coldness of fur, the freshness of ironed cotton, the intoxication of leather when I stuck my nose inside her new handbag, a hint of mothballs and sandalwood.

Now my mother was dead. I had killed her. I was a slayer of mothers.

I blinked, to get used to the subdued light that diffused from pearl glass lamps shaped like flaming torches. Silver hands thrust from the walls and held them. The wallpaper through which the hands sprouted was pink and red chintz fastened up with silver nails delicate as hatpins. The pleated screens that zigzagged about were covered in matching cloth, as were the little armchairs set in front of them. The screens and the armchairs had silver feet. Parked around the walls were wooden racks, white as bleached bones, crammed with dresses.

My wet shoes left a ribbed trail of mud blots across the pink fur of the carpet. I wandered over to the counter in the far corner, glass-panelled, its bracing columns printed with pink wreaths of beribboned flowers. Its top supported a pile of shallow cardboard boxes, their lids half-open as though someone had recently been riffling through them and not bothered to put them away. Sheets of white tissue paper trailed out, the cuff of a white satin sleeve, the seamed toe of a black nylon stocking, the wrist of a creamy suede glove. Alongside toppled a tower of hat-boxes striped in red and white and fastened with black satin bows. Nearby stood a clutter of scent bottles in ribbed glass, some with silver tops, others with crystal stoppers, and next to them an open china powder bowl on which swam a swansdown puff, silk-backed, with a tiny ribbon loop to pick it up by.

My mother would never have tolerated this disorder, these strewn hatpins, this scatter of tortoiseshell combs, measuring tapes, open pots of rouge, curls of black hat-veiling, disarray of gold lipsticks. She would never

3

have allowed this half-crushed cigarette butt to smoulder in this saucer, these face-powder grains to drift across the flap of a crocodile vanity case, this mascara-smudged face towel to drape itself over the gold-coloured till.

But my mother was dead. I remembered her screams like a saw ripping the air, back and forth, catch of the hooked teeth, tug and bleed. A savage unzipping of sound to announce her dying.

I wandered between the clothes racks, examining their burdens of puckered taffeta and smooth thick satin and crushed velvet. Terylene and nylon. Seersucker and lamé. The rain beat down heavily outside, its swish, swish, hushed by the canvas blinds.

The shop intrigued me. A relic from times past stocked with evening wear for dowagers, cast-offs for theatricals, rich pickings for fancy-dress parties. A magpie haul of beaded, braided, embroidered slips and cocktail frocks. Those two-piece waisted suits my mother had called *costumes*. Those sequined confections she'd referred to as *gowns*. A glorious mix of diamanté and ostrich feathers, flowered *crèpe de chine* and pin-tucked lawn, buttons and ornaments and brooches of carved bone, of ivory, of mother-of-pearl.

A garment in salmon colour caught my eye. I lifted its padded hanger and tugged it out. Flesh-pink chiffon filled my arms, a tight, stiffly boned bodice that stood up above a long, smoothly billowing skirt that curved outwards, down. I held its lightness. A dress that swayed against me. A seductive stranger. A dancing partner. Cut to be full, but with restraint. Both voluptuous and severe. With a single layer of chiffon wreathing the shoulders.

The dress leaned on me. Abandoned, tipsy. I bent my head over it, ran the tip of my forefinger along the edges of the crossover bands of chiffon that swathed the bodice. Crisp and new, as though it had never been worn. It was irresistible. It would be my saviour, my disguise. I lifted it up gently in my hands and looked around for the changing room.

A long mirror, tilted to give a flattering reflection, gleamed on its stand in the opposite corner. Behind it, two of the pink and red hangings were

4

looped back to make a tented opening. I saw myself briefly in the mirror as I passed it: tall and lean, white-faced, bearing the dress like a dead woman in my arms; much too masculine for this soft place.

I stepped into a domed bower lit by a glittering pink glass chandelier shaped like an octopus. The curtains were of pale pink brocade shot through with streaks of coral. I pulled them around me, then undressed, flinging my clothes on to the thick carpet since there were no hooks to hang them on. There was just me, almost naked, and the dress. It waited for me, my second skin.

I raised its airiness and dropped it over my head. Whispery touch of chiffon and gauze, of silk lining, crackle of tough buckram. It slithered over me coolly. My arms plunged out, my head, my neck. I pulled the bodice down, I breathed in and drew up the cold metal fastener at the side, almost pinching the flesh of my armpit. My shoulders lifted themselves then settled.

My large cotton handkerchief and my discarded tie, well stuffed in, did duty for breasts. I smoothed my ballooning skirts, put my hands up to check my hair, drew my licked fingertips along my eyebrows. I kicked off my shoes: too big and heavy. All I needed now was the mirror's gaze. To confirm me. To give me back my new and beautiful self. I stretched out my arms, curved my hands palms downwards, and carefully picked up my skirts, like two baskets of eggs I held on the edges of my hips. Monkey-armed, carrying my huge puffs of chiffon, I tiptoed back into the shop.

– Can I help you?

I thought it was my mother speaking. The voice sounded so like hers. Abrupt, cool. I thought it was my mother addressing me, her corpse rising up, greenish-faced, to reproach me. My mother, that robust ghost.

When I turned round she wasn't there. It was the proprietor of the dress shop who stood quietly behind me, fingering the slick black and white length of the measuring-tape slung round her neck. Her small black eyes regarded me. Her small mouth pursed itself. Her hair was very black, as though poured from an ink bottle, and plastered itself thickly across her scalp. She wore a yellow tweed suit with a short curved jacket and straight skirt, a bulky grey linen blouse whose pleats pouted out over her tight

5

waistband, a little black bow tie. She was short and plump. Her small feet were encased in black lace-ups.

— Madame Lesley, she said: at your service. Lovely frock, that. The kind of thing a debutante would have worn for her coming-out.

I stared at her. She spoke again, more softly and slowly this time.

— Mademoiselle would like some assistance?

She whipped a box of pins out of her pocket. She advanced upon me with her measuring-tape, both hands outstretched to lassoo me, stab me.

— Almost a perfect fit, she said: except perhaps the bodice. A few tucks there, I think. And the length isn't right. A bit shorter would be better.

She brandished the pins. She was about to pinch up folds of pink chiffon, discover my secret, my disguise.

— Wait, I cried: there's something I must tell you first. The reason why I need this dress.

The measuring-tape coiled itself up between the swift fingers and joined the box of pins in one of the palms of the plump hands. The round head cocked itself on one side.

She didn't know I was a murderer. I remembered the yells. They weren't my mother's. They were mine. She'd gazed at me with terror and whispered: you must be mad, there's something wrong with you, you must be mad, you are evil. Her words squeezed my throat. Like hands they struck and throttled me. The words my father used before I left his house were covered in darkness, they scratched and fought under the heavy blanket I'd thrown on top of them. Also they were on me somewhere, indelible. Unlike bloodstains they would not wash off. Word fingerprints.

Madame Lesley shrugged.

— Tell me about it, she said: while I do the fitting. Now then, let's see.

She crouched at the hem of the dress, folding it up so that my toes showed. A row of pins protruded from between her compressed lips. One by one she nipped them out and darted them into the frock's edge.

Scheherazade had told stories, night after night, to save her life. She made them up. She was a storyteller. I didn't know whether or not the stories that jostled in my head were true, or whether I was a liar. So many

6

different voices chattered inside me: that meant I was mad. I wasn't sure if my stories could save my life or my mother's.

Out of the mad babble inside me I picked a word. I held it like the end of a thread, unravelled, that I could wind as I wove my way into the labyrinth.

— Well, I began: it was like this. It's about love:

FREDDY

I fell in love for the first time when I was ten years old and still at primary school.

This green-doored building at the end of our street in Holloway I entered every morning along with most of the other children from the neighbourhood. Holloway Road was a treeless and dusty roar of cars, cranes, demolition gangs, workmen crouched inside little striped red and white canvas huts brewing tea, but when you turned down the school street you found massive lime trees, a tiny park tucked in between terraced houses, the ferociously neat gardens of Polish and Greek people, their clipped hedges and trained roses and harmonious shrubs, sage green to silver. Stained-glass windows, black and red tiled paths, gabled brick house fronts decorated like red-brown fancy biscuits. It pleased me to live at the other end of the street from the school. The street like a string tied school to home, tugged me from one end to the other. Under the road ran the River Fleet, a bed of gravel the house shifted on. The secret river ran underground. In my dreams a waterfall flowed down the stairs in our hall.

In school I learned to chant my tables for half an hour at a time, like epic

8

poems, to address a business letter and put an Earl opposite a Countess, to dance Strip the Willow and The Dashing White Sergeant, to embroider in cross-stitch, to play sports and measure rainfall and boil eggs.

– Boys and girls equally, our headmistress Miss D'Arcy sang out at Assembly: should be dexterous in all sorts of activities! None of this metalwork for some and hemming for others. Certainly I approve of hemming. But I hold in addition that proper smocking, appliqué and feather-stitching are arts you will *all* enjoy!

It was my last summer term in her school. The long windows tilted forward, held by cords, let in the smell of mown grass, the far cry of the rag-and-bone man. I sat cross-legged in the back row, next to Martin Wood with whom I had just fallen in love. I kept my back straight and my chin up, as Miss D'Arcy taught us in Deportment. I could smell my feet in their plimsolls, that damp black smell of heat and sweat.

Miss D'Arcy bent her head. Her lower lip ducked forward. She wove together her bony fingers and glared down at us.

– Swimming this afternoon for you dear bigger ones. Hope you haven't forgotten your togs.

Last week, in the green-tiled swimming pool on Hornsey Road, Martin and I were partners to practise lifeguard skills. His hand cupped my chin, I lay back on him, he towed me along. His black hair floated about his white face. Then he tipped me off and dived to swim under the bridge of my legs. When his head popped above the water it was plastered in silky darkness sleek as a seal's. Now that I'd fallen in love with him I was nervous of touching him in case I went red or fainted and everyone would guess why and make my life hell.

Miss D'Arcy believed in healthy minds in healthy bodies and healthy mixing. When the time for the summer and Christmas plays came round she wrote them herself and gave the best parts to the most talented irrespective of sex. Boys pranced in home-made farthingales flirting chicken-feather fans, girls strutted in doublet and hose, carolling up to ambiguous beauties on stepladder balconies, and the panto horse was unashamedly hermaphrodite.

At morning prayers she led us, our six-foot High Priest, in her raw and cracked soprano chant. Catholics, Anglicans, Methodists and Jews, we all joined in. On our behalf she addressed an impartial God with no favourites, a sky-wide umbrella who shaded us all. Half a bar ahead of the rest of us she bawled out the hymns, hands beating the harmonium, then read us chunks of the Old Testament, whatever took her fancy.

Morning Assembly ended with the delivery of physical punishment to outstanding offenders. Boys and girls alike we were whacked. If standing in the classroom corner had failed to mend our manners. If staying in at break had failed to improve our spelling. The weapon varied. Sometimes a sharp-edged pencil-box, stencilled with red anemones, rose up and banged your knuckles held out ready in supplication for the cleansing blow. Sometimes a ruler flexed itself on what Miss D'Arcy delicately referred to as your b.t.m.

– Freddy Stonehouse. Step forward.

My plimsolls crept up the steps to the stage and I had to go with them. Yesterday I'd insisted on joining in the little girls' skipping game. I'd frightened them because I was too eager and too big, jumping in on the slapping rope and knocking one of them out of my way. You're not supposed to play with us, the weeping tot protested, as I danced above the rope her two friends swung. But I'd gone on skipping.

– Freddy, Miss D'Arcy announced: you're a bully.

Today she chose the pencil-box. Her flowered crepe waist was level with my eyes as she administered punishment to my stinging skin. Pain was a red anemone, a clutch of crepe gathers in purple and blue. I looked down at her boat feet encased in plum leather topped with a red bow, then up at her skinny muscular calves. I concentrated on not staring at her moustache. It waxed and waned from week to week, as she tried to get rid of it and it grew again.

– Bad luck, Martin whispered when I sat down again.

– Oh, I assured him: it doesn't hurt at all.

In break he showed me how to draw cartoon faces, which he was learning from a book he'd got out of the library on Holloway Road. I memorized them to try on as masks later on. The cheeky chappie, that's who I'd be. In the swimming pool I clowned and splashed whenever Martin was near me. Nobody spotted I was in love. I made too much noise.

Martin walked with me down the street after school. I hugged my damp roll of swimming things.

– I'll teach you to do three-quarter profiles tomorrow, he offered: if you want.

– Thanks, I said.

We had reached my garden gate.

– 'Bye then, he said.

I watched him lope off, tall and so skinny his joints were knobbles that stuck out, his legs impossibly thin. His shoulder blades protruded through the back of his blue aertex shirt. He was being an aeroplane, arms stretched taut with flattened palms. He wove, growling, to the corner and vanished behind a row of savagely pollarded limes.

– How was school today? called my mother from upstairs as I came into the little front hall.

I wiped my feet on the mat, kicked my way out of my school shoes, put on my slippers. Then I stepped on to the carpet.

– I got hit for skipping, I hollered back: Miss D'Arcy did it.

The Hoover roared and I jumped. My mother's voice was muffled. She had to shout even louder.

– I warned you. You shouldn't laugh at her moustache, poor thing. Freddy you brute!

The carpet in the hall was grey nylon curls, very springy and tough. It bore you up, like a salt sea. I floated to the bottom stair and sent my voice aloft.

– I didn't I *didn't!*

I didn't dare openly laugh at Miss D'Arcy. None of us did. We obeyed her, even when she commanded us, in Elocution & Drama, setting the arm of the gramophone down on to the scratched seventy-eight, to dance into the centre of the room and *be* the dawn! Martin stuck his hands above his head and wriggled his fingers. He looked treelike, also as though he had sent his mind somewhere else. I wanted to impress him, so I swayed, I

11

strained, I flexed my arms and tiptoed forward, I spoke the dawn poem we'd all had to write for homework.

— Voice too far back in the throat, called Miss D'Arcy to me above the harp and trumpets: bring those vowels up and out, on to the tip of the tongue!

Her *régime* worked. I passed my eleven-plus and was awarded a scholarship to the nuns' school. My mother had just converted to Catholicism, so the grammar school to which Martin was going, girls and boys in twinned Victorian redbrick, would not do.

— Good, yelled my mother from the kitchen: we couldn't have afforded the fees. It could've been the secondary mod for you, chum.

The dark-blue and gold tie slipped between my clumsy fingers. The dark-blue blazer was stiff, and too big. Its sleeves scraped my fingertips, which curled round the handle of my father's old briefcase he had given me, testing its stitched edge, curved leather sandwich.

— All very well, my mother called above the thump and swish of the washing-machine: cleverness is as cleverness does. See how far that gets you with the nuns. Bit of a change they'll be from that Miss D'Arcy with her eurhythmics and her Greek dancing and her divided skirts.

The Catholic religion would be a good dose. To get me regular, normal. To cope with my growing pains. The nuns would measure my sprouting sins and bumpy needs, distil me a medicine to ensure my transition into well-behaved adolescence. I wasn't quite sure why the Anglicans wouldn't do as well. I hadn't yet decided to follow my mother and convert. My father remained staunchly Anglican. He had to, for his job, which was working for a firm which designed vestments for Anglican priests. High Church, definitely, but he wasn't *going over*. I heard him tell my mother this late one night. The words came up through the floor. I rarely saw my father as he left so early for work. At weekends he was around, a slender figure with a pointed beard, putting on his camel cardigan then going out to look at his roses and dahlias.

— A very good job he's got, my mother said: and an excellent pension at the end of it.

12

She was on the stepladder, washing the kitchen ceiling. She shook her head at me.

— I suppose you'll have to bother with A levels eventually, she prophesied: one or two. These days you can't even be a dustman without a degree!

Her arm, with the frothy sponge at the end of it, went back and forth like a windscreen wiper. A blob of foam dropped to the lino.

— But you'll walk up the hill to the new school, she commanded: you need the exercise.

My too-soft body dragged itself up the street for the last day of primary school. I was certainly too big to stay here any longer. The little children swarmed in the playground like beetles. If I moved too fast I'd step on them, damage them.

Martin said goodbye casually. He was thinking about his holiday, going camping. He wanted to join the Cadets and learn to fly. Then he was going to be an artist. He had his future mapped out. He put his hands in the pockets of his shorts and whistled and for the last time accompanied me to the gate guarding my house. Warm air moved over my bare knees and forearms, the nape of my neck, I could smell his fresh sweat, all my flesh stood up and cried out, desperate, in terror, my life leaking out on to the hot pavement. The ice-cream van tinkled its music a street away. A scent of petrol and tar.

— 'Bye then, I said.

The convent school perched on top of a hill well to the north of us, a tube ride and a bus journey away. I walked the last bit. Neat rows of detached houses and garages, shrub-sprinkled greenswards, looped-chain fences, fell away behind me. Real countryside began. The road wound between hedgerows. Cows grazed in a tree-dotted field, sycamores shook golden leaves overhead. There was a duckpond at the bend in the road, a stile, a half-timbered pub. I leaned on the stile to catch my breath, studied the meadow with its horse chestnuts, its long grass studded with the loose black coils of cow-pats. I lugged my heavy briefcase on up to the top of the hill, round one more corner, and the convent loomed before me. A high redbrick wall with an arched blue gate set in it, and an iron bellpull marked Visitors.

13

There was a crucifix over the blue gate. The plaster feet of Jesus were clotted with blood like congealed gravy on a dinner plate. An arrow pointing sideways under the nailed feet said School Entrance. I followed the wall and found another blue door. I opened it and went through.

I clopped across a grey asphalt playground walled on three sides by the buildings of the school, then into a damp and dark cloakroom. It smelled of hot floor-cloths and soda, as though it had been recently washed. The wood and iron coat-racks were see-through rows of emptiness. Odd, calm. I liked the lack of people, which made me less afraid.

I pushed myself on, into a corridor windowed on one side, with views of the playground. A cold tunnel with a vaulted wooden roof and flagstones underfoot.

A pointed black door at the far end flew open and a burly nun hurtled towards me. Her raised palms whirled too near my head, and I shrank back.

— Praise be for idiots, she sang out, eyeing my smart new uniform: here's a prize one, dear Lord. School doesn't start till tomorrow, you clot. You're too early.

She guffawed with red gums showing, horse teeth. Her black wings flapped as she shot out a chapped hand and tugged at my blazer lapel.

— What's your name then?

— Stonehouse, I whispered.

— So you're the Stonehouse kid, she cried: and all of us so delighted about your mother coming over. Well, you're keen, aren't you? So let's go and pay a visit to the Blessed Sacrament before you go, shall we? Come along now.

She steered me into another corridor, smelling of floor polish mixed with chalk dust and flowers. Shadowy corners set with plaster statues, blurs of lit rubies I trotted past.

Ahead of us, deep in the building, a bell rang. Clang clang clang. An ugly and urgent summons that stopped my tall companion in her tracks, so that I cannoned into her. She crossed herself and expostulated.

— You must never touch a nun, child. Rule number one. And there's the

Office bell already. You'll have to go. You can't come into the chapel when we're singing the Office. Off with you.

She whisked me back across the playground, bundled me out of the blue door I'd come in by. I heard her creak the bolt across, then her shoes slapped away. I burst into tears. Now I'd have to face my mother's anger at my stupidity. It was she who'd got the date wrong but I wouldn't remind her of that. It was called answering back and made her go even colder with annoyance. I started down the hill, the long haul home. It started to rain.

Soaked through, I made it in through the door and up to the bathroom, puzzled by how queer I felt. When I took off my wet things I found there was blood coming from between my legs. This was what saved me from a telling-off.

Some girls called it the curse. It would have to be kept a secret from my sensitive and fastidious father. I knew all about it from the magazines and from the dour hints my mother had let drop. But I'd assumed it couldn't possibly happen to me.

– Oh lord, exclaimed my mother, when I leaned over the banisters to announce the news as she came in from shopping: I do call that a bad sign, *I* didn't start till I was much older.

I swigged hot Marmite with my lunch. I was in a delicate condition, like when I returned from the dentist after having a tooth out, with a gap that tasted of metal and blood, an absence gouged in the gum that my tongue couldn't ignore. Marmite was a comfort. A thin black drink that easily scalded the roof of your mouth. Salty liquid tar.

My mother didn't have lunch because she was on a diet. She went out into the back garden to hang up the wash and I read her copy of *Housewife and Home*.

The models in the magazine photographs wore little tip-tilted hats, elbow-length ruched gloves, hostess gowns, high heels. They were trussed in girdles and suspender belts and pointed brassieres and sheer nylons. Their shaved armpits gleamed with roll-on deodorant and their mouths with lipstick applied from blunt gold sticks. They were elfin, apart from

15

their large uplifted bosoms, they were creatures of frailty and dainty hygiene. They had small feet.

A famous actor picked out his favourite hat from a double-page spread of about fifty photos of models all wearing different styles. He chose a little black one with a swirly polka-dotted black veil. There's something so feminine and mysterious, he explained: about a woman in a veil.

Another piece was about being *soignée*, which meant perfectly groomed from tip to toe. A man had cried out when the woman author of the article, elegant and chic as could be in a new suit and hat, met him for lunch in a restaurant in the West End. Darling, he cried out in horror as she advanced to greet him: your *nails*!

These men's concern awed me. They knew what real women should be like. They felt that standards should be kept up. Women could easily go sloppy and slack, or like Miss D'Arcy.

My father, I knew, sympathized with the men in the magazines, for his life was dedicated to the Ideal of Beauty. At work he was surrounded by lengths of brocade and silk unrolled from fat bales then flung across tables for the designers to stroke and finger. The colours of the Liturgy: green and purple and white and gold, with scarlet and black for special occasions. Robes for Anglican priests who were very high. They looked exactly the same as the vestments worn by Father O'Dowd in the local Catholic church to which I sometimes accompanied my mother. An ugly concrete shell despised by my father, pews in sharp light wood, no mystery or glamour, too modern, too bright.

My father loved glamour as part of Beauty. He loved looking at pictures of film-stars and singers, and listening to his opera records. All round the house he hung Old Masters of beautiful nude women, lying on rumpled silk beds surrounded by slaves and flowers. The only room in the house unadorned with these pictures was the kitchen where my mother, since her conversion, had set up a shrine in one corner. Here she kept her rosary, a bottle of holy water, her calendar showing famous places like Fatima and Lourdes, her miraculous medal on a silver chain, and statues of Our Lady and the Sacred Heart, all on a little shelf covered

16

with a paper lacy doyley and set with candles and flowers like an altar.

– Typical convert behaviour, my father said: more Catholic than the Pope!

But he did go with my mother to buy a new outfit for her to wear to church. A two-piece suit in dark-red velvet, with a frilly lace blouse and a tiny velvet hat like a plum. Over the plum my mother cast a black mantilla. Behind it her eyes were soulful. My father's hands flew about, expert. Twitched the skirt into place, pulled the hat forward, set the pochette bag at exactly the right angle under her arm. She pirouetted while we watched. She was little and slender, my mother. She was pretty and young. Smiling as she was now, with her curly dark hair pulled back into a chignon, she looked like one of the models in *Housewife and Home*.

– I'm not having you go over to the Romans, my father said: without doing me credit!

That was in the summer. Now I had to do my mother credit, and not let her down in my first term at the nuns' school.

I went back the following day. The right date, this time, for the start of the academic year. Now I was Frederica Stonehouse, in a bulky tunic and pullover, and with a stash of sanitary towels in a brown paper bag in my briefcase, masquerading as a packed lunch in case anybody looked.

The first day of term began with Mass attended by the whole school, in the chapel, which was large as a church, dark, and which smelled of flowers, incense and wax polish, heavy and sweet. We new girls packed the front pews. Blue felt kneelers on the red tile floor. I peered about at the brocade curtains drawn back to frame the side altars, the racks of blazing candles, the myriad statues of saints dressed in real clothes of silk and lace. An invisible organ pealed plaintively. Kneeling at the far end of the front pew, I was able surreptitiously to advance my hand and stroke the white feet of the statue of the Virgin Mary which stood on a low plinth in the space between the pew and the painted and gilded wall. The Virgin wore a white silk veil anchored by a crown of silver stars, a white silk cloak dotted with gold over a blue dress. She held both her hands out to me in a gesture of complete love, complete acceptance. She bent her eyes on me very sweetly.

17

She was my mother and she loved me. In this voluptuously sacred place I was at home.

Sister Benjamin's cane tapped the back of my legs. She was the nun I had met the day before and clearly she had her eye on me. I hastily turned and faced the main altar, where the priest was fiddling about with a chalice and muttering to himself.

The chapel had a special part, on the right-hand side of the main altar, behind a metal grille, reserved for the nuns. I could just see them, if I swerved my eyes behind the grille of my own fingers I had put up against Sister Benjamin's gaze.

The nuns confused me. Penguins, I'd heard the other girls call them in whispers, as we filed in for Mass. They seemed a third kind of person, not male or female nor really anything in between. They could not be judged by those men in *Housewife and Home* so anxious for women to be glamorous and *soignée*. They lived concealed inside their long black clothes. Their clothes-houses. They were in disguise. But *what* they were I could not be sure. They were not like me, I was certain of that.

— I'm going to convert to Catholicism and become a saint, I told my mother on my return from school.

— What? she hollered from the other side of the bathroom door: what's that you said, Freddy?

I knelt down and pressed my cheek to the glistening cream paint. A plywood panel between her and me, like the confessional I had seen in the school chapel, that she hid behind, like the priest. To reach her my voice had to compete with waltz music on the radio, the flushing of the lavatory, the gurgle of the water spilling out of the bath.

— I want to be a saint, I whispered to the keyhole.

Her screech of laughter scrubbed my ears.

— Pull the other one! *You* be a saint! Oh dear me. Priceless you are. Just wait till I tell your father!

The keyhole cupped by my hands was a pursed mouth refusing me. Its brass mount tasted cold against my lips. The key to the bathroom was long since lost, which was why my mother played music inside at her bath-time

18

to alert me to keep away. She usually had her bath at four, ensconcing herself in scented steam, with the newspaper and the radio to hand, just before I got back from school.

My father bathed in the mornings, once he'd returned from his early dip in the local outdoor swimming pool, then went off to work. He had a special rough towel that he rubbed himself with, that no one else was allowed to use. It was good for the circulation and toned up the skin. My father took care of his looks. He trimmed his black beard to a sharp point just under his chin and snipped the hairs inside his nose. He Brylcreemed his hair into waves, and splashed on eau de Cologne. He shaved his upper lip very gracefully, gliding the razor so that he didn't nick himself, flicking blobs of lather into the hand-basin with one deft shake of the wrist.

He often shaved twice a day, because by tea-time, when he was home from work, the shadow of a moustache would have appeared above his lip. He wore a paisley silk dressing-gown to shave in. The suit he wore for work was put away, and he would come downstairs in soft, loose corduroy trousers and one of his cardigans, wine or amethyst in the week, camel at weekends. Sometimes he wore the dressing-gown all evening, if he was tired, with a silk scarf tucked into the neck. He would lie on the settee and listen to a record of opera with his eyes closed. *Aïda*, turned up very loud.

He heard me slink past the bathroom and called to me to come in.

– Shut the door, silly, he said: don't stand there in the draught. Sit down, silly.

I parked myself half on and half off the chintz-covered box where we threw our dirty clothes for the wash.

– Be careful with those nuns, he said: don't believe everything they tell you. They like to fill the heads of young girls with nonsense. Especially about sexual matters. Take it with a pinch of salt.

I stared at the bath-taps. He was wiping his white soap moustache from his lip with quick precise strokes of his razor. I saw his gestures out of the corner of my eye. But I didn't want him to catch my eye in the mirror. I stared hard at the taps.

— Sex is a great glory, he said: do without it and you're done for. Neurotic. Nuts.

— I don't want to marry and have children, I told him.

— Oh, children are no bother, my father said: they bring themselves up. You give them a roof over their heads, clean clothes and beds, food, and that's it. They're little animals, that's what they are, they don't need anything else.

My father pressed a fluffy white towel carefully on to his face.

— You're still very young, he said: once you've lost some weight you'll develop a lovely figure, I expect. A real stunner you'll be turning into. You'll feel differently once you're a bit more grown-up, you'll see.

I knew what real stunners were from looking at the pictures of naked ladies in the magazines my father thought he kept safely hidden under the sample swatches of ecclesiastical silk and brocade in the bottom drawer of his bureau. I'd found them one day when he and my mother were out at a cocktail party and I was going through the bureau to see what he had in there. Bored, wanting to discover something interesting. The magazines were in black and white, and showed women bursting out of their skins. I saw why my mother called nakedness my birthday suit. The captions referred to señoritas, nymphs, bathing beauties, pert soubrettes. The words rolled across my tongue and fizzed like sherbert. I couldn't believe I would take after my mother and turn into a swan. It was too late. I was already too large. Too tall and too *fat*.

For tea we had corned beef fritters. They were oblong, the shape of the tin they'd come out of. The pinkish-grey meat, shredded then pressed back together with white fat as glue, was cut into slices, and fried. To follow we had sponge cake coated with raspberry jam scattered with desiccated coconut, tinned mandarin oranges, and custard.

— I'm going on a diet, I told my parents.

My mother dived back into the kitchen to fetch the pepper and salt. My father always forgot things when he laid the table. All through the meal she popped up and down, fetching serving spoons, place mats, the glass jug of watery orange squash.

20

– If you really want to convert, Freddy, she yelled through the serving hatch: you'll have to undergo a course of special instruction, like I did.

I could call the dieting fasting, I reasoned, and use it to show God I was serious about becoming a saint. I decided to give up cake, biscuits, sweets, puddings, orangeade, tinned fruit, and sugar in tea and coffee. Instead I would eat greens, particularly spinach, without grumbling, and tinned sweetcorn ditto, and I would take my cod-liver oil capsule without threatening to be sick. And I would make myself an altar, like my mother's in the kitchen, only in my bedroom. An altar to Our Lady. I would enlist her help, get her on my side.

My mother's wasn't a real altar, as she herself pointed out to my father the day she put it up, more of a repository for objects of devotion. A real altar, she explained to him as he stood jeering gently, was what the priest said Mass at in church. It contained the relic or relics of a saint, put there when the church was first consecrated. The relics were built in. You couldn't see them when you knelt in your pew praying. On the Continent, she said, they went in for relics in a much bigger way. In Italy, for example. They felt proud of their relics of saints and displayed them for the faithful to revere. Not worship, she stressed. Revere. But relics had miraculous powers if touched. They made ill people well again, for example.

– I know that, my father said: I'm an Anglican, don't forget.

My mother had one relic she had bought in the Catholic shop up in the northern end of Holloway Road. It was a splinter of the True Cross, sealed in a lump of resin inside a clear plastic box. It was so precious she didn't risk keeping it in her kitchen shrine where anything might happen to it. She carried it in her handbag so that she had it with her at all times.

Thinking of her handbag gave me the idea for how to collect some relics of my own for my shrine to Our Lady. Since Our Lady, I had already learned from the nuns, was taken up body and soul into heaven at her death, it would be a waste of time for me to imagine I could have any of her bones on display. But I thought I could include some marks of her passing, some traces of herself that she had left behind. So I foraged, to begin with,

21

in my mother's handbag, while she was busy with the ironing, then in the bathroom and her bedroom. In the end I had a fine assortment.

An old aspirin bottle filled with some of my mother's bathwater, scented with Blue Grass bathsalts, looking cloudy rather than dirty.

One of her handkerchiefs I took from the box in the bathroom, a pink one, with a crust of dried snot in the corner.

A piece of cottonwool, twisted about a hairpin, that she'd used for cleaning her ears and that I got to before she threw it away, clotted with yellow wax.

Some of her toenail clippings I rescued from the frilled waste basket next to her dressing-table.

Hairs from her eyebrows still clinging to the tweezers.

A nest of dark-brown hair pulled from her hairbrush.

I put the relics inside a brown paper bag at the back of my underwear drawer. Next time my mother came in to poke about, she'd be fooled. The searchlights of her eyes, swivelling over the contents of the drawer to check for order and neatness, would flash past what looked like a cache of sanitary towels modestly wrapped. I didn't want her to find out about my altar until I was ready to show her.

In the evenings, when I was supposed to be doing my homework, I drew sketches of the statue of Our Lady I was going to make. The plaster ones in the shop up Holloway Road were not beautiful enough. I tried copying some of the women in the pictures hung around the sitting-room walls. Most of them were too plump for the Virgin Mary, and of course didn't have clothes on. They were pink and fresh and tight as uncooked sausages. I couldn't see why it was all right to have them on the walls just because they were painted, why photographs were ruder and had to be hidden. But none of these women would do as my model for Our Lady. She had to be smooth, not curved, almost flat. Like a boy.

I was thinking of Martin Wood when I went out of the house on Saturday morning, after my first week at the nuns' school, and there he was, lounging against the gate-post.

My father had gone down Holloway Road with my mother, to help her with the shopping. I'd refused to go with them. People stared and giggled at my father pulling the wicker shopping trolley on wheels and with another basket crooked over his arm like a handbag. They smiled at his gilt-buttoned blazer and his camel cardigan displayed underneath, at his slender hands, at his pointed beard. So I stayed at home.

I went into the front garden because it was hard being on a diet. I felt faint with hunger only an hour after breakfast and longed to race into the kitchen and ram my hand into the blue storage jars in the larder, scoop up currants and raisins and sultanas, cram them into my mouth. I decided to swallow fresh air instead. I opened the front door and saw Martin Wood standing waiting for me. The sun was shining on his hair and he was outlined in radiance, like an angel, a dark glory, suntanned and black and glittering.

— Oh hi, he said: I was just passing.

— Hi, I said.

I remembered the sociable words my mother used to the Catholic priest when he came visiting.

— Oh do come in, I said: won't you come in?

— OK, Martin said: but I can't stay for long.

Love and hunger mixed up inside dissolved the solid edges of the privet hedge, the path, when I glanced at them so that I wouldn't stare at Martin's face too greedily. A flash of brown skin, that lock of black hair that fell foreward over his eyes, merged with light dazzling gold on bitter green leaves, red and black tiles like squares of chocolate, melting.

— I've got something to show you, I said: come in and see.

He hesitated. Hands in pockets, lower lip slightly stuck out, glancing at me through his long lashes.

— My parents are out, I said: there's only me at home.

He shrugged.

— All right then.

He followed me through the grey front hall with its bristling mat like an angry dog, its bamboo coat and umbrella stand. I opened the sitting-room door. Black fingermarks marred the glistening cream paint around the silvery grey aluminium handle. I hadn't done my Saturday jobs yet, the first of which was cleaning the lounge. Front room, my mother said. Sitting-room, said my father. Girls at school said lounge.

I watched his glance flick over my mother's collection of paper fans, ivory elephants and rhinos, brass ashtrays and inlaid boxes, that decorated the mantelpiece and occasional tables, the tall corner vases stuck full of plumy grasses, the three-piece suite in nubbly grey tweed draped with white linen antimacassars, the upright piano with my parents' wedding photo on top in a silver frame. Next to it was a photo of me taken at school the year before, frowning and pig-faced. When he saw it he'd despise me for ever. He'd not want to come upstairs and see the precious relics I'd collected for my shrine. He'd shrug and leave and I'd never see him again.

– Holy shit, Martin said: take a look at these!

He jerked his head to indicate the pictures on the wall.

– They're Old Masters, I told him: my father really loves art. He says he can't live without beautiful things around him.

Martin walked with a bit of a swagger, head thrown back, whistling under his breath. He was definitely older-seeming now he was at his new school. He examined the pictures close up, one by one. He pushed his eyes into pink breasts and stomachs. He opened his mouth and the tip of his tongue caressed nipples as plump as cherries. His wedge-shaped face was intensely alive, concentrated into two burning points of looking. He gleamed with something between scorn and fascination.

I loved him and I wanted to give him everything I had, every treasure I possessed, though my hands were empty and I lacked riches and could think of nothing that was mine to give. He was here with me, I breathed his air. I had to keep him from going, as he'd threatened five minutes ago to do. I had to find something to show him that would make him stay. He would not be interested in my paper bag of relics, in my shrine that was not yet real. He was not a Catholic and would not understand.

– Oh, those pictures are nothing, I said: you should see these.

My father's bureau stood in the bay window. The key to the bottom drawer was in the little tortoiseshell box where he kept paperclips. In a trice I had half a dozen magazines out and was scattering them across the floor.

— Here, I said: what about these!

Naked ladies lay on the carpet with their legs apart and looked up at us as though we were grown men. We squatted on the carpet the better to study their dishevelment, their open-mouthed looks both anguished and ecstatic, their poses and gestures, their fur bracelets, their spike-heeled boots. We dived down into their glossy black-and-white pool that the light rippled over, we swam into their paper arms, we fidgeted in their celluloid laps and peered up between their thighs into that place I had no name for and which dissolved, the closer you got to it, into a dance of black dots.

— I'm not their real child you know, I told Martin: I'm convinced of it. I've found out. I'm adopted.

Martin switched his eyes from the naked ladies to me. Now at last I had his attention. Puzzled, wary.

— So who are your real parents then? Do you know?

Any minute now metal would scrape and click outside beyond the hall as my mother's key struggled in the front door lock. Any minute now my parents would heave in their baskets and string bags of food and mended shoes and dry-cleaned clothes and discover us. They were approaching too close. I needed them to be far away.

I glanced back at the magazines. Subtitles to the photographs gave the models' names: Claudine, Reinette, Colette, Albertine.

— French people, I improvised: from France. My name isn't Stonehouse at all. They just found me when they were out walking one day, it was like this:

FÉLICITÉ

Félicité found the egg stone on the beach at Etretat, when she was walking there with her fiancé Albert at low tide.

They were pacing to and fro on the lowest ridge of stones, just a yard away from the water's edge. To left and right of them the steep white wings of the cliffs arched out, enclosing the little bay. They leaped forward, white bridges, into the blue-green sea.

– Not a bad little place, this, Albert declared: now that it's been smartened up a bit.

All through Félicité's childhood Etretat hadn't changed. Narrow alleys edged with gardens tiny as pocket handkerchiefs separated ancient half-timbered houses. Newer villas tucked themselves in alongside, with balconies overlooking the sea, tiled and shingled roofs. Then the railway opened, and the little fishing town became an elegant resort busy with visitors from Paris. On the white promenade a new hotel had been built, and a Casino, and several glassed-in cafés. In or out of season, the business end of the beach stayed exactly the same. Félicité could have sketched it with her eyes shut: the black iron winching-up machinery, the dragged-up fishing-boats and nets, the coiled heaps of hairy ropes, the bundles of wicker lobster-pots.

Her fingers rubbed against the small drawing book in her jacket pocket. Too chilly to sit down, Albert had decided: better to take a walk. Félicité lifted her face into the sea wind, which blew fresh and sharp. Albert kept her arm linked into his as they trudged along. Under their feet was the dry clink, clink of pebbles rubbing together, mottled and pearly and striped. Rounded stones, pale grey, lavender, white. Pure smoothness, worn into eggs you could weigh in your hands, fill your lap with. Every day of the holiday Félicité returned to her aunt's hotel with her hands clasping her pockets heavy with stones collected on the beach. She arranged them on the windowsill of her room, just as she'd done as a child. Before going to bed she stroked them, bent her face close to them to smell the sea on them. She chose a different one each night to put under her pillow. When she was married she supposed she would have to stop doing that. It was rather too childish after all.

The waves drew back quickly over the shingle, leaving a trace of froth. Then the filigree wetness, fragile silver, disappeared, and another wave broke in its place. Félicité could smell fish, the drying seaweed that lay about in rubbery clumps, tar. Nearer to hand was the scent of Albert's eau de Cologne and hair-oil, sprinkled drops, a buttery slick, lemons and spices and flowers mixed. She turned her head away a little, wanting to smell the breeze, its salt tang.

Albert squeezed her arm as he spoke. He kept her close to him.

– On Monday we should go into Le Havre and look at some of the houses on the list the agent sent me. We should make a start.

Félicité put on a bright smile. She could see it, glittering like a brooch, two enamelled lips framing bared white teeth. Carefully she raised her free hand in its tight kid glove to touch the velvet cap she wore tilted forward over her eyes. Too sudden a gesture would split the fragile seam. She drooped her eyelids. She made her voice sound neutral.

– It must be exactly the right house, though, and that will take time to find. And I haven't got everything we need yet. There's still the dinner-service to choose, and the bed-linen isn't finished.

Albert's new job, as clerk to the engineering department of the Le Havre docks, meant a move for both of them. Félicité wanted to live on the quayside, as close to the sea as possible. Albert was determined to start married life outside the noise and smoke of Le Havre, to buy a house high up in the green seclusion of Sainte Adresse, the new suburb halfway up the steep cliff backing the port. Brand-new redbrick detached, he wanted, with fretted white wood gables, ornamental stonework around the front door and windows, a neat white fence, rows of marigolds on either side of the gravel path. Inside would be clean shuttered rooms, harmoniously furnished, papered in immaculate modern style.

Félicité ran her tongue over her lips. They tasted of salt. The only room she could imagine, in this house they hadn't yet agreed upon, was the linen-room, where she'd keep all the sheets she hadn't yet finished hemming.

– You can't get married without sheets, she said: we'll have to wait until they're done.

A square blue room, long white muslin curtains at the windows. No pictures or ornaments. Just one big carved pine cupboard with double doors, to which she alone kept the key, pinned close in her apron pocket.

Her little world that waited for her. Paper-lined shelves, strewn with sprigs of rosemary and lavender, bearing neat piles of linen.

White sheets, pillowcases, bolster-cases, counterpanes.

Tablecloths, table-napkins, traycloths.

Face-towels, towels for the hands, the body, the feet. Face-cloths.

Drying-up cloths for glass. Drying-up cloths for plates, for saucepans.

All reposed quietly in place, uncreased, gleaming white, in this sweet-smelling interior where no moth dared venture. Félicité counted and checked her treasures. She smoothed and stroked them. She tugged the piles of folded linen into exact alignment, with a last fond pat. She wanted to place herself next to them, inside the cupboard-house, still, undiscovered, in the darkness that smelled of cedarwood and herbs, of sun and wind. Folded flat as a page from a sketchbook.

She closed the cupboard upon her bounty, her white treasure, and locked it. Before dust fell in, or the sun's rays, or cooking smells, or Albert's eyes.

Albert's moustache scratched her cheek. Albert's hand moulded itself to her shoulder, pressed it.

— Darling, your parents have promised us a bed. All we need is a couple of pairs of sheets to start with. Everything else can wait till after we're married. You refuse to start married life with my mother. So let's look for a house.

Brown interiors smelling of yesterday's boiled chicken. Brown wood, brown sticky varnish, brown wallpaper with a mauve pattern. Small dark rooms tight with ornately carved chairs, vases full of dusty dried flowers, too many photographs and engravings in frames that made you think of funerals, too many carved dressers and sideboards full of ornate china that was too good to be used. Cramped. Tufted carpets your feet tripped up on. The ache of boredom. A thin-lipped atmosphere of drawn curtains, criticism. Marriage in that house would be a brown mouth that bit you primly then swallowed you alive. Albert loved his mother. They would have to go and see her every Sunday. Félicité would be given instructions on how to supervise the maid of all work, and she would be held responsible for Albert's health and well-being, the proper functioning of his liver, the exact performance of his bowels.

Félicité wriggled her arm out of Albert's grip. She squared her shoulders. A wooden canoe shot over a wave, its two passengers laughing. Their wooden oar skimmed the water. High above, the gulls lay on the air, then pulled away, swooped and dived.

Two dozen soup plates, Félicité counted to herself: two dozen dinner plates, dessert plates, side plates, two vegetable tureens, one soup tureen, three serving platters, one sauceboat. They had not yet bought the sideboard to keep it all in. Where the plates would shelter, clean as the haloes of saints, safe from the hands of men who were clumsy, too quick, who broke things.

— Hmmm, darling? said Albert: shall we?

— What? Félicité said.

This pink silk jacket she had on today, for example. Brand-new, part of her trousseau. Against her mother's advice she'd brought it with her to Etretat, wanting Albert to see her in it, wanting it to be admired by the guests in her aunt's hotel. Herself in it, tightly swathed in pink silk, trussed in pink silk cords. Like a salmon thrashing and beating before its breath finally goes. Ribs of silk holding in her breath. Falling winded like a boxer against silk ropes. Then Albert had spilled mayonnaise on it, lunging at her with the silver ladle rather than letting the waiter do it. Her aunt had dabbed at the stain with soap and hot water but it hadn't come out. The jacket was ruined.

Albert hadn't realized how hurt she was. She loved mayonnaise with poached salmon but after that she hadn't been able to swallow a mouthful. Just to show him. He'd gone on stuffing in tiny golden fried potatoes, and she loved those, and green beans in cream sauce, and he'd called across the table: have a glass of wine, old girl, that'll cheer you up. Now he was trying to be so nice, but it was a bit late for that. He should have thought of that before.

She moved a step away from him. He saw the red flush that surged into her averted cheek and settled. Her mouth wobbled, then compressed itself. Her shoulders went rigid. She presented Albert with her profile, staring out to sea, pretending to admire the view. She had halted so suddenly that other passers-by strolling along the beach almost bumped into them. A few amused glances were cast their way, a few smiles. The handsome young couple. The lovers' tiff.

Albert felt half exasperated, half admiring. He liked Félicité's spirit, her sudden moods of defiance that passed so quickly, her childlike whims and gaieties. Pandering to her was a part of courtship. He understood the reasons for her irritability. Waiting to be married was hard on them both. She'd calm down once she was settled. He would stroke her into docility. A house, babies, all that would absorb her energies.

So he forebore to tease her out of her sulks. He kept her on a loose rein. He let her be. He enjoyed watching her fuss with a loop of hair that dangled from underneath her floppy cap, pinning it back into place. The hairpin

slipped and slid. Félicité drove it in. The tight cloth of her sleeves restrained
the rounded curves of her upraised arms. Her blue eyes shed two tears then
sparkled again. Her waist was tiny, stiffened and subdued by the sharp lines
of her corsage. Her hips and breasts swelled out, released, above and below,
like the curves of a flower coming into bloom. Like a gladiolus bursting
from its sheath. A pink one. Albert smiled. His mother grew gladioli along
the edge of her kitchen garden. They were his favourite flowers. He
gripped his lapels, and inhaled the fresh sea breeze.

   – Come along, sweet. Let's walk a little more.

   He dug his fingers into her silk arm, steering her past a low outcrop of
black rocks. She lowered her firm chin, her aquiline nose. Her fair skin had
reddened in the hot afternoon sun. The sachets of lavender sewn into the
armpits of her lace blouse could not prevent the smell of her perspiration
escaping: pungent, vanilla-like. She cried out.

   – Don't walk so fast. I've stubbed my toe.

   She looked down at her cream-coloured kid boot. She glanced at the
stone her foot had struck, bent down to pick it up. She clasped it in her
gloved fingers for a moment, then held it out for Albert to see.

   Just a bit of fallen cliff, pummelled into pebble shape. Pockmarked and
scarred, crusts of yellow in its crevices. Félicité turned it over, and Albert
saw that it was half of an egg-shaped stone that had split. Half of a stone egg
cut open lengthwise, with a solid white, a solid yolk. At its centre was a
lump of golden quartz. Glittering. Like marzipan, oozy, as though you
could scoop it out with your fingertip and taste it, sweet and warm yellow,
the crunch of sugar grains.

   – They're all like that inside, Albert said: it's just that this one's cracked
open, that's all.

   He took it from her and held it. He closed his fingers over its rough
curved coat, then stroked the smooth inner skin of the exposed centre. It
was heavy, and cold. Damp still, smelling of the sea. He handed it back to
Félicité.

   – Here. I don't want it. Have it for your collection.

   She slipped it into her pocket. The stone nestled at the bottom of the little pouch of silk. It was round as the inside of her palm. She put her fingers around the outside of her pocket, feeling the hardness of the stone through the softness, carrying it.

They wandered on, this time going right to the end of the beach, towards the *caloges*, the beached boats with thatched tops that the fishermen used as huts for storing their gear.

Albert felt his fiancée's lack of response to him. Now he was a little aggrieved. What had he done this time? He tried to enter her mood. He used her sort of language.

– How picturesque, he exclaimed.

He was looking at the group of women seated on the beach around a wide hollow half-full of water. Red-faced, hearty women, dressed in black. The daughters and wives of fishermen. Busy doing their washing. Beating the clothes on the stones and then rinsing them in the clear stream.

– It's called La Fontaine, Félicité threw over her shoulder: freshwater, an underground stream from the Grand Val that comes out here. That's why the women gather here to do the washing whenever there's a low tide.

– Look, Albert interrupted her: there's that English fellow. How odd, I thought he told us he was going into the country today to paint.

– Monsieur Mannot, Félicité echoed.

She remembered the unused sketchbook in her pocket. She gazed enviously at the half-dozen artists who had set up their easels on the stretch of shingle just below the washerwomen. Cliffs and *caloges* framing them one way, the sea the other. Grey and white and black, a tossing line of turquoise, patches of green.

One of the painters looked up. A bare-headed young man in a faded blue blouse and trousers stained with sea water and paint, he was of medium height, with a thin face and quick, restless eyes.

Albert shrugged.

– He's not a proper artist, that one. Just playing at being a bohemian. A fishy character if you ask me. You should take more care about whom you allow yourself to meet.

The young man rose from his camp stool, wiping his brush on a paint-encrusted rag he pulled from his trouser pocket. What had once been a piece of white cloth. An old vest cut up, perhaps, or a section of nightgown, possibly a large handkerchief. No longer the sort of cloth that took its place in linen cupboards, next to respectable pillowcases. Too ragged and stained, too much smelling of turpentine. In time, that was what happened to sheets. They wore out. You turned them sides to middle and made a new central seam. You patched them. Then in the end you tore them up and used them for rags and one or two might end up on the beach at Etretat, in a painter's pocket. If your husband was a painter, that is. Or if you were yourself.

– I wanted to sketch today but it was too cold to sit still so long, Félicité cried: yet here you are, hard at it. How's it going? I know we mustn't look till you say we can.

She carefully said *we* because she could feel Albert's boredom and annoyance eddy out of him like a smell. The painter smiled at her. He came closer and shook hands.

Albert considered that Félicité was behaving like a little girl. She exaggerated. Coquetting, with a pout and a smile. She clasped her hands and rocked from foot to foot on the pebbles, a child on an outing asking for a lemon ice. Curls of hair escaped from under her cap and flew about her face and neck. In her striped blue and white skirt and pink jacket she was rosy, pearl-tipped, eager.

– Calm down, Albert remarked to no one in particular.

– My landlady's horse went lame, George Mannot said to Albert: I took it as an omen not to go.

Albert bent his eyes towards the young fellow from his muscled height. He pulled at his moustache and said nothing. The painter wiped his hands on the rag he held. Much too late. He had already touched his dirty palm and fingers to theirs. He chatted on. Really, what a little monkey the fellow was.

– I'll go tomorrow, in the *diligence*. There's an old manor house I want to sketch, just beyond Gonneville.

Félicité felt hungry. The sea air had revived her appetite. She wanted to

33

bite into a good chunk of cod with her strong white teeth, to tear off a piece of fresh bread and mop up the fish juices with it. She wanted to gouge mussels from their shells and tip them into her mouth, thick yellow curls, frilled bags, plump and yielding, little bursts of taste, white wine and parsley and sea water.

— What a coincidence, she cried: we were thinking of driving out tomorrow, weren't we Albert, to go and look at houses.

— Monday, Albert said: not Sunday. That's what I had suggested. And modern houses is what I meant, my dear. New ones.

— So we're free tomorrow, Félicité said: we could come with you. I'll bring my sketching things.

Albert fished the tourist guide from his pocket, consulted the index, flicked over the small pages.

— Nothing, but nothing, he read aloud: ever happens at Gonneville, and yet everyone goes there.

George Mannot laughed. Above their heads the gulls whooped and sailed on tossing currents of air. In the changing light of late afternoon the sea was like blue milk. The hill of pebbles in front of them glistened blue, the cliffside was golden.

Two of the nearby washerwomen seized and wrung out an enormous sheet. They dropped it, a twisted coil, into the wicker basket standing nearby, then took up another. Their rolled-up black sleeves revealed the muscles of their brown arms. Their faces gleamed with sweat. The fronts of their dresses were open for coolness. Félicité watched Albert's eyes flick across those sun-reddened triangles of breast, those round throats, those sturdy calves and ankles so openly displayed beneath the kilted-up skirts.

The washerwomen took no notice of the group of painters and tourists staring at them. They talked and laughed among themselves in *patois*. One woman sang as she pounded and squeezed the heavy mass of wet linen. A small hoarse voice. She was using the song, they could see, to put energy into her arms and hands, which struggled with the dead weight of sopping cloth, lifted it with effort, kneaded it. Her torso twisted like the wet sheet. Her shoulders strained and knotted. Her waist, whalebone-strapped in an unyielding black bodice, bent this way and that. Her forearms tautened, tensed.

— Wonderful, George muttered: wonderful.

A fishing-boat was riding in out of the glitter on the horizon. It drove straight at the beach, tipping up and down over the swell of the waves. The washerwomen saw it too. They dropped the thick tangles of wet sheets into the basket, stood up, stretched. They un-settled themselves, like a whirl of gulls. They flapped their wings, called to each other in harsh voices.

— Boat arriving. Come and help haul it in.

The group of painters had to stop work. Their models abandoned their position. The quaint composition broke up. The washerwomen pulled each other up the shelves of the beach, slipping and sliding on the pebbles in their wooden sabots. They applied themselves to the iron arms of the winch, trudging round and round.

George started to whistle. He put his easel and folded stool under one arm, slung his canvas bag of painting things over his shoulder, the rolled sketches sticking out at one end. He nodded to the other painters then turned back to Félicité.

— Come and dine with us at my aunt's hotel, she said: she has lots of artists staying during the season, she'll be charmed to meet you, won't she Albert?

She sent her fiancé a glance of blue-eyed affection. She beamed at him with trust. Albert pretended that he was convinced by this show. To reveal his annoyance would be to let her triumph. He braced his shoulders, made a stiff little bow.

— Do, my dear fellow. Delighted.

George's smile cut past Albert, aimed at Félicité, like an arrow in an archery competition thudding confidently into its mark.

— I'm sure you'd love to see the manor house. Why don't you both come with me? We'll take a picnic lunch and eat in the orchard.

— And I'll sketch too, Félicité said: I'll do a watercolour for my aunt, she'll like that.

She was delighted. *We artists*, she thought. It was good for Albert to see how at home she was with all kinds of people. It didn't matter that George lacked changes of clean shirts, that his collar was frayed and his trousers dirty. Artists were like that. Splendidly careless. They were, by definition, not bourgeois. Their moral code did not concern itself with little things like clothes.

She tapped George on the arm. It was a gesture which, as an engaged woman, she could confidently make without its being misunderstood. That was the other thing about artists. They treated you as a person. They were not afraid to make friends with a woman.

– Come along, boys, she cried: or we'll be late for dinner.

She swept them before her, up the beach.

The hotel *Au Rendezvous des Artistes* was in the main street leading to the *place*. It was a medieval house. Félicité liked to imagine how it had stood there, squashed in between its tall stone neighbours, for centuries. Its façade was of wood, pierced by small mullioned windows. The steep roof pitched down very low. All the timbers were carved with little beasts. Lions and cats crouched half-hidden above the windows, tiny twisted men somersaulted at the ends of beams, grotesque birds stepped in a frieze above the main door. Here and there, under the eaves, were small blue and white tiles stuck in decorative patterns, and the catches for the shutters were cast in the shape of little people, their heads blurred with green paint.

George whistled.

– I shall be delighted to see inside. I walk past here every morning and roar with laughter.

Félicité frowned. She loved the little carved animals that you could see only if you looked hard for them, the wobbly glass in the windows that distorted your view, the worn step at the threshold, the ancient rafters.

She thought: what do you know about it: You're a foreigner.

She compressed her lips. She gathered up her skirts with one hand and approached the door Albert was holding open for her. She smiled at him and went in, George following close behind.

The dining-room at the hotel was warm. Puddles of yellow light reflected off cutlery and glass, the shiny fronts of engravings hung round the pink walls. The floor felt springy, it invited you to tread lightly over its planks of golden wood. A scent of ham and roasting lamb hung in the air. George sniffed loudly and smiled. Félicité watched him take in the white cloths, thick and starched, that dropped stiffly over the edges of rows of square tables, the baskets of bread set ready on the sideboard, the battalions of cruets drawn up alongside the piles of plates.

Madame Godin's glance, practised and quick as the beam of a light-house, swept over George's boots, cuffs. As she advanced to greet them, her hands smoothing the tiny frilled muslin apron she had tied over her black velvet dress, Albert sprang forward so that he reached her first. He kissed her on both cheeks, grasped the hands that had reached for the apron's minuscule pockets, pressed them. He stooped over her and whispered in her ear. She was a little woman, plump, with the shine of youth still on hair and skin, with sharp blue eyes. She laughed and tossed her head at Albert's whisper as though it tickled her ear, shook hands with George, kissed Félicité. Then she went with small quick steps towards the swing-door that separated the dining-room from the serving area connected to the kitchen behind.

Thick curtains masked the long windows, dark pink to match the walls. The shades of the gilt and china lamps were creamy yellow. Félicité fetched an extra chair for their table, set it so that George sat between her and Albert, facing in, at the end. She collected up extra knives and forks, a silver stand bearing glass bottles of oil and vinegar, and brought them over. She fussed prettily with napkins and spoons. George sat down, yawning. He snatched up a piece of bread, tore it in two, crammed the bits one after the other into his mouth. He caught Félicité's eye.

– I'm starving. Sorry.

For someone so thin he could certainly eat. Rillettes, saucisson, lamb chops, each dish vanished in a twinkling. Albert looked on without comment. He poured more wine into their glasses and watched George throw it down. He helped himself to another couple of chops and lifted his eyebrow at Félicité.

She awoke early next morning to that grey darkness that meant rain.

Summer grey, misty, like a starched poplin dress gone soft in the creases, almost blue. Sleepily floating between darkness and light in the silvery-grey room, she heard the rain attack the roof just above her bed, where the ceiling sloped down to the wall, pattering briskly on the shingles. The rain drew itself around her, the hush-hush of gossamer.

Félicité pulled the quilted cotton coverlet closer. She listened to the rain which built her a secret house she alone inhabited. A house of rain with soft grey walls, with a melting roof and a sliding floor of earth. As a child she'd loved rain, darting out into it half-clothed, dancing and waving her arms, whenever she got the chance. Before she was caught, dragged back inside screaming, soundly slapped. Filled with a mad gaiety she had never felt since. Now, drowsing in her dawn bed, she thought that the room smelled of sea air, and that the sea was filtering in along with the light, and that the rain brought with it also the smell of animals, of steamy barns, of plants growing, of crushed fruits.

She woke again, hours later, to her aunt's bang on the door, the clatter of the maids carrying breakfast trays, buckets of hot water. Now the sun was up, colouring gold slits between the edges of the closed shutters, the drawn curtains, falling in bright slices on to the red tiles of the floor. Shavings of sun which were warm under her toes when she pattered barefoot to throw open the shutters and dispose the red woollen curtains in their daytime folds.

Wrapped in her blue and white kimono she sat on the edge of the bed and watched the maid jerk across the room with two cans of water, arms held out just enough so that the two brass pails didn't bang her thighs, jaw set with concentration. She didn't know this maid's name. A country girl, she looked. Small pale-blue eyes, frizzy hair twisted into a knot on top, hefty arms and legs.

Félicité wondered. *Was* it this one? Seen for a few seconds last night after Albert winced, got up to go in search of another bottle of wine, George emptied his wineglass too fast, he didn't understand that in France one sipped, he wasn't genteel, that's why she liked him, wasn't it. But this girl, now, a glimpse of her snatched as the swing-door into the serving area was pushed open by Albert's shoulder then hurriedly shut. Her face tinged red with cooking steam, her eyes bright, palms held out away from the bosom of her black dress and white apron bib. A rush of dark air reached Félicité at the corner table where she sat, the smell of chops frying, sizzle and sputter as drops of blood jumped out into the hot fat, a stifled cry, a giggle. She could imagine the rest of it. Two white hands casting the red chops marbled with fat into the black pan, two red lips parted, the meat seared and scorching as the juices caramelized, Albert's hand diving under her lifted skirt, a splash of cognac over the chops, then Albert reappeared with a smoking silver dish piled with cutlets and a bottle of wine tucked under one arm. Félicité smiled and smiled as she took up the spoon and fork and dug the silver prongs through the crackling skin into the red flesh under-neath.

Félicité watched as the maid gingerly heaved up the cans of water, one after the other, tilted them on the edge of the little bath, poured them in. She yawned. At home in Paris, the maid was too elderly to carry heavy weights. Félicité had to carry her own hot water upstairs, and that of her parents. Here she could perch on a soft quilt, lean back on a pile of cush-ions, watch this farm girl clank back across the room with an empty can dripping under each arm. The door shut behind the maid and Félicité sprang up.

Hair loosely plaited and pinned on top of her head so that it wouldn't get wet, she knelt on the scratched enamel of the bathtub. A worn patch gaped black under her right knee. She fished the soap from its tin box on the floor beside her, let it pop from her fingers and thumb, from one hand to another. A green sliver of scented fat that might just last the holiday. Then she'd squash the new cake on to it so that none went to waste. She rubbed the slippery wafer across her skin. An odour of ferns rose up. She dropped the soap back into its dish, scooped up water in the china jug that stood next to the soap-dish, repeatedly rinsed her shoulders and arms. They gleamed through the rush of wet. She hummed aloud with pleasure.

Then she stood up, toes braced on the narrow base of the tub, where it started to curve upwards towards the sides. She stepped carefully out, hoisting one leg after the other, balancing on one hand gripping the enamel edge. She stood, dripping, on the cotton rug, and seized the linen bath sheet hung over the back of a chair. She patted herself all over, then twisted the sheet around her, tucking the loose end in under her arms. Like someone in an exotic picture. A slave girl, perhaps. Or a lady in the harem. Proud, with flashing eyes, and point-toed slippers.

She sat down on a small red armchair round as a tomato, unpinned her hair, shook it out. It fell, dark brown and curly, below her shoulders. Now Félicité was being a mermaid on a rock, luring sailors to their doom. In one of those artistic pictures where the careful arrangement of hair and draperies meant that the model wasn't really all that nude at all.

The mermaid reached out a languorous hand for her hairbrush, which was lying on the wash-stand. She looked up and saw Albert watching her from behind the half-open door.

She kept still. She could see herself, swathed in the white sheet, bare-shouldered and flushed, in the little mirror tilted above the wash-stand. She could see herself as Albert did, motionless, one hand stretched out to grasp the hairbrush, the other laid flat against the front of the sheet to make sure it did not fall. She met Albert's eyes. She stared back at him, holding her quick intake of breath. He was pink-faced, his fingers flying up to tug at his moustache. Then, with a click, the door shut behind him and she was alone again.

Albert had gone out early and hired a carriage. At all costs, he had declared over dinner the evening before, he wished to avoid travelling in the *diligence*, crammed in with a load of strangers and noisy tourists. Félicité had laughed at his fastidiousness, shooting a sidelong glance at George and sighing exaggeratedly. The young painter had shrugged and spread his hands.

– Well. If you're paying for it I'm not going to argue.

The carriage turned out to be a clumsy, old-fashioned affair that wouldn't have looked out of place in a farmyard. Swept out and dusted by the hotel's potboy, however, furnished with rugs and cushions by Félicité's aunt, it was pronounced viable.

Albert was in a bad temper now because Félicité had taken so long getting ready that they were setting out more than an hour late. This meant paying the driver extra, for wasted time. Albert went to the foot of the hotel stairs and shouted.

— Come *on*.

Félicité came sauntering downstairs. She was feeling rather pleased with herself because she was not wearing a corset and could therefore move and breathe exactly as she pleased. She had broken the strings with which the corset was laced up, broken them in two places, so that putting it on became quite impossible. To conceal her scandalous condition from her aunt she had enveloped herself in a light mantle she normally wore only for going to church.

— To keep the dust off, she explained: these country roads are bound to be filthy.

She leaned into the cushion padding the cracked leather of her seat. She smiled at everyone.

George sat forwards, behind the driver, who wore a red woollen bonnet, a blue jacket, and a sort of skirt over his baggy trousers.

— He's an off-duty fisherman, Félicité whispered: George, you must certainly sketch him. Such a picturesque costume!

Albert sat next to his fiancée, separated from her by the picnic basket covered with a green and white cloth. He had selected and packed the lunch together with Félicité's aunt. In the dim, cool back kitchen of the hotel he had walked to and fro, lifting the covers off dishes, prowling into the larder, the meat safe. He had chosen slices of cold roast pork, pieces of veal in thick golden jelly, some little chicken-liver tarts, a waxed cone of cooked sausage and gherkin, another of ham and *salade russe*, a bag of cherries, another of greengages, a ripe Camembert, a round loaf. Madame Godin had been reluctant to send her niece off unchaperoned on this jaunt into the countryside. Albert, tucking the cloth around the top of the basket, had been reassuring.

— I'll take the most perfect care of her. Now you know I think of you as practically my mother-in-law. So you must believe me!

She consented. She let him take a jar of strawberries in brandy, and a twist of paper filled with almond biscuits.

— When you get to the Blanquet farm just beyond Gonneville, she instructed him: stop and buy some cider. Theirs is better than anything I've got here. And don't forget to be back in time for evening Mass.

The carriage jolted out of Etretat, into the Grand Val. Leaving the coast and the cliffs behind, they entered a green landscape rising towards gentle hills. The road ran between pastures dotted with grazing cows, fields of oats and barley, potatoes and sugar beet. A green steam rose up from everything, as the sun increased in power and warmth. The smell of the carriage, of dust and chaff and rotting leather, was not so unpleasant out in the open air. It mixed with the smell of the salty breeze, the fresh smells of mud and cabbages and manure.

Albert was taking the young Englishman through a sort of catechism. Did he shoot? Box? Do gymnastics? Train with clubs?

— None of those, George replied.

He smiled at Félicité. He leaned back in a parody of indolence, straw hat tipped over his eyes, legs crossed, plaited fingers resting on his brown corduroy waistcoat. With one slender booted foot he tapped the easel and wooden box half-tucked under his seat.

— Painting wholly occupies me during my summers here, every year. I've no time for sports. Except for falling in love with local beauties of course. Irresistibly pretty, these Cauchoises. Such a way of holding themselves! Such truly astonishing bonnets!

The carriage was lumbering past a row of thatched and half-timbered cottages. On the steep green bank in front of these a group of farm girls, dressed in their Sunday clothes, sat chatting. They displayed their families' wealth. Gold-threaded shawls over white chemises and black bodices, blue and red striped skirts, laced black slippers, and high starched and wired head-dresses, towering like the curved horns of mythical beasts, trailing ribbons of elaborate lace from their unicorn tips.

— Oh yes, lovely girls, Félicité cried: really sweet, don't you think so, Albert?

— Turn here, Albert commanded the driver: go through the centre of town.

Gonneville was a large village as empty of life as the guidebook had predicted. The church bells ringing out indicated that everyone was hidden under the ugly spire, attending High Mass. The market square was deserted, the bars were shut, the streets were clean and quiet. In five minutes they were through the village and out on the open road again which ran, narrow and straight, between rows of feathery poplars.

— Don't let's bother stopping at the Blanquet farm for cider, George suggested: the people at the manor farm have plenty, I know.

— It's inhabited, then? Félicité asked: you know the people?

— The owners don't live there, George answered: but I made friends with the farmer and his wife earlier this summer. I was staying there for a while, making sketches. Before coming to Etretat.

Albert laughed out loud, showing all his white teeth. Strong like soldiers, marching in two rows.

— Only a foreigner would imagine he could make friends with peasants. Really my dear fellow you're impossibly romantic.

— Stop here, George told the driver: we'll walk up.

Rusty iron gates stood open between stone posts. They were sunk in deep grass, made fast by brambles and weeds. What had once been a drive was now a mud track, rutted and potholed. At the end of it they could see the manor house, a large half-timbered building whose base was of stone, with a slate roof.

Félicité shrugged, and began picking her way up the drive. The left side of the house was flanked by a double row of beech trees. Through a wide gap cut in the high bank on which the trees were planted they entered the farmyard. Félicité gathered her skirts well above her ankles, to make sure they skimmed the mud. With her other hand she waved off the two dogs that came running out to bounce around them, barking and wagging their tails.

Albert stood beside her. She leaned on his arm and inspected their surroundings. The farm buildings were massive as a fortified hamlet. Ancient

43

barns were arranged around three sides of a square. The farmhouse was one side of the entrance they'd come in by, a couple of tumbledown cottages on the other. The farmhouse was well tended, at least. The patches of plaster showing between the lathes were freshly done in creamy yellow, the thatched roof was thick and trim, white curtains hung at the windows, and earthenware pots of begonias were set on the windowsills.

A young woman, hands on hips, emerged from the doorway to meet them. A sturdy young woman with scraped-back blonde hair and small eyes, her body wrapped in a decorated shawl, a high bonnet perched on her chignon, its strings tied under her chin in a big bow. It was obvious that she knew who George was, that she was expecting him. Her face held the possibility of a smile. She stood still and erect, very dignified.

— Now I understand, Félicité whispered to Albert: now I see the inspiration for his paintings!

She and Albert were back in league again. Excluded by George's embarrassing familiarity with these people, his air of belonging. The young woman was certainly rather pretty, if you liked that style of beauty. Félicité refused to participate in the introduction George was clearly about to make. She nipped Albert's arm and stepped back, pulling him with her. She nodded and grimaced in the direction of the doorway, then took Albert to inspect the dovecot in one corner of the farmyard, an octagonal structure in alternating layers of stone and brick with a conical thatched roof, the bricks patterned in lozenges of red and white. Grey and white and brown birds flew in and out of the openings under the eaves.

— They look like pigeons to me, Albert complained: are they supposed to be doves, or what?

He tugged at his tawny moustache. Pouting and very handsome he looked, the sunlight glinting on his bright brown hair and beard. Félicité squeezed his arm.

— I don't know, she said: I'm a stranger here. In this quaint rustic world!

Albert's shiny new boots were clotted with mud. He was too hot. He was hungry, and he was thirsty.

— George is just play-acting, he burst out: what a buffoon that fellow is!

44

George emerged from the dark doorway of the farmhouse, a bottle under each arm, another sticking out of his jacket pocket. The blonde young woman followed him. She stood close to him and said something that made him laugh. Then she laughed too, and clapped him on the arm. Understanding, her gesture said: at home. Félicité half-closed her eyes. She peered at the chickens scratching nearby in the trodden earth, their darting necks and pecking beaks. She noted the carriage driver plod past, tugging the weary horse towards the shade of the tall beech trees.

George came towards them grinning.

– All right. Let's eat!

Albert fetched the rugs and cushions from the carriage, then went back for the picnic basket. Félicité wandered ahead, empty-handed. Albert never let her carry anything. She dangled her palms in the warm air as she walked, she fluttered her fingers. She made straight for the centre of the orchard, wanting to pick a bunch of wild flowers to decorate their tablecloth. She fell into brambles and nettles. George rescued her. He settled her on the thick plaid blanket under the least gnarled of the apple trees, and made her lean back into a fat cushion. She sat docilely. He brought her a fistful of dock leaves and made her wrap her stinging hands in them for five minutes.

– There's an awful lot of insects flying around, she fretted: look at that huge buzzing thing.

George poured a tumbler of cider and held it out.

– This will take your mind off your troubles.

Félicité swerved her eyes from the large dried cow-pat only inches from the rug. She sipped from the thick-rimmed glass. The cider was so dry it was almost harsh. Yet it ran down her throat smooth as honey, a fierce golden warmth.

Albert dumped the picnic basket in the centre of the rug and sat down beside her. He tossed off a glassful of cider. He drank a second one thirstily. He poured himself a third, sighing with pleasure.

George opened a second bottle. Made of opaque green glass, dusty and unlabelled, crusted with cobwebs, which he rubbed clean on his sleeve. A net of wire, twisted into a loop at one side, kept the cork in place. An exploding mushroom that shot out, a gush of thin white foam into their glasses, then the stream of cider, pale gold.

— Pierre makes the cider himself, George said: the cider-press is in one of the barns back there, he showed it to me. When I was here before.

Félicité dug her fork into a piece of cold veal clotted with jelly. Next she took a mouthful of ham and *salade russe* whose coat of mayonnaise shone thick and glossily yellow. Out here in the open air, she had to admit: the food did taste good. The flavour of sunshine and fresh grass had got into it somehow. She pointed her fork at George.

— But why are you so interested in these people? she asked: are you going to paint their portrait or something?

Her empty, oil-smeared plate on her lap, she put her hands palm down on the sun-warmed roughness of the rug and blinked across at George who sprawled opposite her. She felt it was like being in a painting. The green backdrop, the play of sun and shadow across the green and white tablecloth, the three languorous bodies. And, in particular, herself, the apex of the human triangle. Chin raised, showing the curve of throat and cheek. Her blue and yellow blouse unbuttoned because of the heat, its linen frills tumbling anyhow. Her hat laid on the grass. The faint breeze stirring the curly tendrils of her piled-up hair.

— I'm going to put all my sketches together in a book, George said: glimpses of rural and maritime life in the *pays de Caux*, that sort of thing. For a foreigner, you know, the local colour is so charming, so picturesque.

He was laughing at her, she was sure.

— Félicité, George coaxed: beautiful goddess of the picnic basket, I can tell you all these things because I know you'll understand. You care about pictures. You've been a real friend to me.

He fished a handful of golden greengages out of the basket and laid them at Félicité's feet.

— Don't mind me teasing you. Have one of these. They're delicious.

— Albert is asleep, Félicité whispered.

Her fiancé lay on his back on the far side of the rug, in the shade of the green apple-boughs, his head pillowed on his rolled-up coat, one hand flung up across his sun-reddened forehead. He looked so peaceful and young, so worn out, as though he'd run for miles before collapsing in this orchard swarming with flies and bees. Two empty cider bottles lolled beside him. The flies were busy on the rim of his glass.

— It's so hot, Félicité said: that would be most refreshing. Thank you.

She sat up feeling lonely and shy, like when she was a small girl being taken out to tea with children she didn't know. She put out a finger and touched the glowing roughness of the greengage. She took it up and bit into it delicately, then cried out as juice spurted over her mouth and chin. Hurriedly she put the whole fruit into her mouth at once, spat the oval stone into her palm, wiped her sticky hands on the grass.

What should she do now? George was watching her, smiling.

— It's so hot, she repeated.

— Sssshh, George reproved her: pity to wake Albert. Sensible fellow, isn't he, taking a nap.

Félicité was hunting for her handkerchief, so she didn't answer. George pulled her to her feet.

— Come and see the house. It's much cooler inside. Hermine gave me the keys so that I could show you around.

— It's not her house though is it, Félicité protested.

— She keeps an eye on it for the owners, George said: while they're away. It's practically empty. They're going to restore it, Hermine says, and then furnish it. Come and see the room I've been painting in. You'll love it.

Félicité hesitated. She glanced at Albert, then at her skirt. It had some crumbs on it, which she busily dusted off.

— I don't know, she said: perhaps I ought to wait for Albert.

— You're not scared, are you? George asked: of being alone with me? You of all people! I didn't think you were so conventional.

— Oh I'm not, Félicité hastily reassured him: not at all.

His face showed that she'd hurt his feelings. She felt her own face go scarlet. Such vanity, to suppose that George was interested in her in that way. Such a lack of trust in him. She hastened after him out of the orchard and on to the grassy open space in front of the house. He waited for her to catch him up. His manner was perfectly friendly, as though to say: don't worry, think no more about it.

The air was very still. Thick and close in the afternoon heat. No sounds, apart from the cooing of the doves. The dogs must be asleep.

Hermine darted past in the distance, carrying what looked like a basket of eggs. She was going towards her cottage. She saw them standing together in front of the great stone doorway and gave a friendly wave.

Félicité's hands did not want to wave back. They hid themselves in her pockets. One touched her little sketchbook, the other the egg stone, which she had brought with her, she didn't know why. She looked down at her feet, half-buried in long grass, weeds with little yellow flowers that smelled pungent, bitter. She saw the corner of a paving-stone. She'd almost tripped on it. She curled her fingers round the egg stone, held on to it.

— Fifteenth-century, George said, gesturing at the wide carved doorway: beautiful, isn't it?

He fitted an ornate iron key into the lock of the wooden door. He pushed the door open, and held it for Félicité. She released her breath, glancing over her shoulder towards the distant orchard. A scrap of scarlet was one of the cushions from the carriage, a patch of blue was the rug. Her fiancé was invisible. He had melted into a composition of greens, streaked with blue and white, dotted with red. Félicité walked quickly past George and into the manor house.

The darkness and coolness came at her forcefully. Like a slap in the face. Like moist hands pressing themselves on her skin, around her waist. She shivered then relaxed. The darkness had a smell to it, dust and apples mixed. Hermine had been storing the fruit from the orchard in here. Félicité's eyes made out the pile of wicker trays, half-covered with an old blanket. She drank in their musty sweetness. Then she followed George up the wide stone stairs, and through the double wooden doors at the top.

This was the main bedroom. At one end stood a fourposter bed, all its hangings and draperies gone, its mattress covered by a white spread. Above the massive stone fireplace was suspended a washing-line, with what looked like men's handkerchiefs pegged to it. Against the near wall was a tall *armoire* with an ornate pediment, in grey-gold pine. Like a small castle inside the heart of the house. Guarding what? Félicité hesitated. She felt like a thief, prying about in someone else's private place. But she supposed the absent owners wouldn't care. Would they? It was exactly like going into a church in the afternoon, when no one was about, and stepping into the forbidden sanctuary, opening the tabernacle, prodding the Host. Unthinkable. George was watching her hesitate. He was smiling. Félicité touched the silk-smooth wood of the *armoire*. She opened its door and put her head inside.

It was empty, except for a single steep pile of sheets, which looked surprisingly clean, on one shelf, and, peeping out from behind them, what looked like a nightshirt. Recently laundered and ironed. A faint smell of rosemary lingered. Félicité traced the edge of the shelf with one finger, leaned her forehead against the inside of the door and shut her eyes.

George's voice was close to her ear. A warm brush of sound across her cheek.

– Hermine's got a cupboard a bit like this, in her house. She got it for her trousseau, full of clothes. It's a wonderful list of things, what she got to get married, like a poem. I made her recite it to me over and over, so that I could learn it by heart. Listen.

The room smelled of resins, of burnt pine branches, as though a fire had recently been lit in the grate. This was where George and Hermine sat and talked to each other. Of course. On this bed, here in this room. Their secret place, which Félicité had discovered. Like a playroom for children. They could play at being grown-ups exchanging secrets and not be found. It was not too serious.

– Four dozen chemises, George recited: two camisoles in coloured wool, two chintz bodices, one feast-day bonnet in cloth of silver, six coifs, six caps, two cloaks and two mantles, two red and three blue skirts, three coloured linen skirts, ten muslin *fichus*, twelve pairs of drawers. All that's to last her the rest of her life. What have you got in your trousseau, Félicité? Is it as fine as Hermine's?

George's hands placed on her shoulders turned her round. Inside her

49

there was a slight ache, and she wanted to bend over it, to wrap her arms around herself. The room wasn't dark enough. She couldn't hide. George could see her, because he'd opened one of the shutters. He was staring at her. Hot white sun fell on to the floor. It was violent. Félicité thought it would scorch her feet. She backed away, George following her. Now she was cornered. They stood facing one another next to the high bed whose bare posts and rails stuck up towards the ceiling like the masts of a sailing ship.

She recovered herself. Because George's voice was as light as though they were chatting politely to her aunt in the hotel in Etretat. What was the matter with her! One glass too many of cider, sitting too long in the sun outside, and she felt swimmy and weak, and all hollow inside.

– Hermine brought a spinning-wheel with her when she married Pierre, George said: and a bed, and a linen-chest. What does your *dot* consist of, Félicité?

She couldn't understand why he was telling her these things. His voice came from a long way off, talking in some kind of code. She was supposed to smile, to show she understood, but she saw herself in the villa at Sainte Adresse, imprisoned behind its wall of new bricks, shining bright and ugly in the glare of the sun. The flowerbeds had sharp corners that hurt your eyes, and were planted with single blooms that stood to attention in the raked earth six inches apart. Indoors, Félicité stumbled from room to room, opening one cupboard after another to check on linen, porcelain, silver. She washed dusted wiped polished then she put everything back and locked the door. While Albert's mother watched to make sure she did it all correctly, in the right way and the right order she'd been shown so many times. Everything she'd always wanted would be contained in that house. She would never want anything again. For the rest of her life she'd be there. Then she'd be dead and that would be the end of that.

– Félicité, George said: you're so sweet.

The bedpost loomed up behind Félicité. She liked its hardness in the small of her back. It ensured she stood up straight and didn't double over. Her insides clenched and unclenched. Her knees were melting and wouldn't hold her up.

50

– My dear girl, George said.

His brown eyes were tender and bright. His breath smelled of cider. A pleasant smell, sugary-sharp. He kissed her, and her stomach convulsed, electric. His fingers traced the outline of her face. A caress, warm and light, that gave her back edges, solidity, saved her from blurriness. As though he were going round her with a pencil prior to filling her in with colour.

– You're looking so pretty, Félicité, George said: sit there on the bed, sit down, and let me draw you. As a memento of a special day.

Everything felt far away, unreal: the stuffy room, the smell of wood shavings and dust. She watched George pull the sheets from the cupboard. He threw one on to the bed, flapped it, spread it. The scent of fresh air and sun-dried linen fanned out, renewing the room, waking it from tiredness, dullness. He hung a second and a third sheet around the bedposts. The sails on a boat. A tent of white draperies. Félicité sank down into billowy whiteness. Smooth under her hands. Softened by years of laundering, years of being used, lain upon. Husbands and wives wearing them out.

George sat down next to her, on the edge of the bed. He smiled at her.

– You'll have to lend me your drawing things. I've left mine outside.

Félicité propped herself on one elbow, then the other, poked her hands into her pockets. She drew out the egg stone from one, a crayon and her sketchbook from the other.

George leaned forward and took the stone.

– That's nice. Look at all that lovely quartz in the middle.

You would never take him for a proper Frenchman, because his English accent was there in his tumbling speech. But she liked the sound of his light voice talking French. He pretended he spoke it like a native. But his odd pronunciation had a certain charm.

– You can have it if you like, Félicité said: I'd like you to have it. Keep it. It's a present.

– Thank you, George said.

They stared at one another. Then George reached down and pulled off Félicité's boots. He opened her clothes, with enjoyable slowness reaching for buttons, hooks, buckles. She lay back, savouring the touch of his

51

fingers, confident and deft, as they pulled and unwrapped her layers one by one.

This was the great moment of her life. She was about to give herself to her lover, just like all those women in books. She arranged herself in a pose of controlled languour, like a model in a painting. One arm up behind her head, the other laid lightly across her rucked-up skirts, the splayed fingers of her hand resting on the dip of cloth between her parted knees. She stared at George as he came to lie beside her, still fully dressed, his shirt open at the neck showing a triangle of brown skin with a bloom of red on top of it.

– Darling Félicité, he murmured: thank you.

She felt so proud of herself. Taking a risk. The greatest risk; with the unimaginable experience just beyond it like a fall off the cliff. She hung in empty air. She felt for his hand and held it. His mouth moved over her breasts, nudging the skin to respond, leaving a trail of kisses.

She pulled his head up so that she could kiss him again, she wrapped her arms and legs about his and embraced him heartily.

George took his mouth away. He stroked her face, he smoothed back a lock of hair from her forehead and tucked it behind her ear. A patient gesture, non-demanding, that she liked. She could show her own eagerness, sprint towards him.

– It's our afternoon, George whispered: let me love you, darling girl, let me.

A propeller fan lazily turned its blades deep inside Félicité. A little shiver of pleasure took her by the throat, then erupted downwards. Her hips lifted themselves, she wanted to get a good grip on him, rock and slide to and fro on the tumbled sheet already warm from the heat of their bodies pressed close together. We'll have to be quick, oh hurry, we haven't got much time, but do it do it, I want you to, I so want to know what it's like.

At first it was like a scuffle, when his hand slid up and in. Then they relaxed, as George's hand began very gently stroking her, finding a rhythm that pleased her. It didn't hurt, which surprised her, it didn't hurt at all. That ache she had felt earlier was now being taken care of, massaged deeply and strongly. She felt like one of the monkeys she'd seen in the zoological gardens, clambering nimbly up a tree with arms and legs, she hung on to George with all of her, she stared into his eyes that stared back, she was so warm, something very sweet was building itself inside her, like a fountain about to be turned on. She lost consciousness of everything but George's hand and eyes, she surged forward in a great flow, the heat and sweetness tunnelled through her, she was the beach, she was the underground river, she was La Fontaine erupting with a loud cry then thrown back on the pebbles.

An intense sneeze of the body. That's what it was. She lay flattened by it, thighs squeezed together to contain it, smiling. George lay next to her, smiling too. But now he was up, smoothing down his hair. His face was flushed. He sat on the side of the bed and leaned away while his fingers did up the collar of his shirt which had come loose.

Félicité clasped her hands behind her head. A kind of listening was going on inside her, as the warm sweet wave receded, she heard it ebbing back, the slither of sea water over shingle. She pressed her thighs together again, once, twice, she yawned.

– I'm not sure really, she said: that I do want to marry Albert, you know. I've been thinking I'd like to be a painter, like you.

She heard with precision how George laughed. It marked her, a nick from a blade, it stung her skin, sharp. A short laugh, quick and impatient.

She heard him school his voice into exasperated tenderness.

– My dearest Félicité, of course you'll marry Albert. The lucky fellow. And in the intervals of being adored by him and giving him squads of very fine children I've no doubt you'll find time for some watercolour sketching in that tiny sketchbook you so coyly keep tucked in your pocket.

He straightened up and turned to her. He took her hands in his and kissed her cheek.

– Darling Félicité. Thank you. You've made me very happy. Thank you. But come on. It's time to go now.

Félicité held on to his hands.

– You don't understand. I want to be free. Like you.

53

George pulled his hands away and stood up. He walked over to the door. He was angry, she could tell from the set of his shoulders. His voice was ashamed. He flung words at her like pebbles and she ducked. He was red-faced. Somehow it was her fault. Something she should have known.

The wooden latch banged. She heard his feet tap across the uncarpeted stone floor of the landing outside, then die away as they reached the staircase. She imagined him descending it, running down, tramping step by step further away.

Sticky dampness between her legs and on the sheet. She reached down with her handkerchief and wiped herself. She brought up, on the flimsy lawn, a bright red dot. She dabbed again. Hardly any blood at all. Just enough to be a sign, a red mark on the white sheet.

She knew she should get up, roll down her skirt, button her jacket and blouse, and follow George downstairs, but she couldn't move yet. Something had felled her and she was weak. She'd forgotten what George had said. Already it was gone.

The redness was red like her period. At home, when what some girls called *les Anglais* and some *her flowers* arrived each month, she used rags from old sheets, torn up, to staunch the flow, which she had always secretly liked. Redness first inside her then outside, her skin was a frail boundary, a line between redness. She soaked the reddened cloths in buckets of cold salted water, then rinsed them, wrung them out, hung them to dry in the kitchen. You were not supposed to wave those flags from balconies.

She saw the thick plait of wet sheets the washerwomen wound and twisted on the pebbled beach between the arching cliffs, under loops of crying gulls. She could smell sea water and oysters and mussels. Her joined hands made a hinged and fluted shell, opening, closing, opening, holding the memory of the egg stone inside. She was lying in a house of white sheets, the sea wind blowing in on her through the gaps between the soft walls, crevices of linen crusted with salt. She could stay here all night long and the sea would rise and fall around her pebbled bed with its white walls of mist and spray. The hung white sheets around the fourposter were blank as canvases that the painter hadn't yet made a mark upon. Blank as pages in

54

a notebook. There was a red word and she knew it. She could write it, paint it, whether George were with her or not.

She knew she was lying. She wasn't brave at all, she had no talent, she was just a silly young woman who'd thrown herself at someone who despised her now for what she'd done, how would she ever get home, what would she say to George if ever she saw him again. What about Hermine, if she came in and saw her like this, what about Albert. She buried her face in the pillow: I'm alone, I don't know who I am when I'm alone, I'm frightened, I don't know what to do.

The wooden latch on the door clattered up and down. The door flew open then banged shut. The noise of breathing. She lifted her head and looked. Albert. He was dazed, his hair rumpled and his cheeks red, he'd lain too long in the sun then woken up abruptly, he must be feeling awful, mouth dry and stomach sour, after drinking all that cider in the middle of the day. He was wiping his hand across his eyes as though he couldn't believe he saw her there, pressed away from him as far as she could get, into the white sheets, deep inside the great bed, back against the wall. She saw his face when he understood what she'd been up to, she couldn't scream when he lunged at her, she knew he meant to kill her, she was convinced of it, she held the knowledge deep inside that that was what men did in such situations.

— No please no please no, Félicité whispered.

Albert was hurled on top of her like a boulder fallen from the cliff, thwack, on to someone lying far below asleep on the beach unable to move or get out of the way. His furious eyes woke her out of her stupid reverie, paralysed with terror, his hand was forcing her legs apart the other was yanking open the buttons on his trousers.

— No no no she whimpered before his hand hit her across the mouth to shut her noise then stuffed in a corner of sheet to gag her and he shoved himself into her as rough as possible grinding at her bones tearing her skin pumping his hatred into her and a stream of filthy words into her ear. He was gasping, his hands clutching her shoulders and shaking her as her body arched convulsively away away only to be brought back beaten with the flat of his hand, he was crying too, they were both drowning in salt water. There was no one to save her, no one, not Hermine, not her aunt, not the washerwomen on the beach nor the chambermaid in the hotel, there was no one to help her. All she had were words, crashing inside her head like waves on to the beach, words which filled her and blotted out the pain, lifted her up, high up, till she could see herself lying crying on the bed while Albert rolled over and sat up, words which relentlessly told her a story about evil:

EUGÉNIE

I t was widely recognized, amongst those of her acquaintance privileged
to witness her indefatigable battle against evil, that Madame de
Dureville, like her mother before her, was a saint. Her confessor once
declared at an ecclesiastical dinner that he knew of no other living female
who so perfectly exemplified feminine virtue, who so triumphantly rescued
her sex from the degradation of Eve, and who so beautifully combined the
humility proper to true womanliness with the greatness of soul and the
worldly wisdom that understood the need to give generously towards the
charitable projects of the local clergy.

Madame de Dureville's natural sensibilities being inclined towards
melancholy, it was not, perhaps, surprising that her religious temperament favoured penitence and penance over ecstasy; devotion and expiation
over revelation. Scrupulously obedient to her confessor's advice, she bore
with exquisite meekness her husband's often-expressed irritation that she
could not provide him with a son. She endured successive miscarriages with
heroic resignation and fortitude, and, in between frequent and debilitating
pregnancies, all of which, alas, except one, ended in disaster, in renewed

disappointment and grief for the sorrowing parents, she occupied herself with attending the sacraments and fulfilling the duties consonant upon a Christian woman of her position.

She instructed the illiterate peasants on her husband's principal estate near Rouen, where she dwelt, in their catechism, so that they might receive Holy Communion and be confirmed. She visited the sick and the dying in all the cottages round about and helped them prepare for the imminent encounter with eternity and anticipate its awe-stricken contemplation. She prayed endlessly for the unrepentant and the wicked amongst them. She cut up her maids' old clothes for the inhabitants of the local hospice. She sent copies of texts drawn from the Gospels, printed on cards at her own expense, to the Magdalens, rescued from a life of squalor and vice, who gave birth to their children in the penitentiary run by the holy Sisters of the Sacred Sigh.

These orphans Madame de Dureville helped to clothe and feed from her own purse, denying herself the luxuries due to a woman in her lofty social position in order the more bountifully to supply the needs of the sin-begotten babes she snatched from their mothers' evil example and transplanted into this Catholic vineyard watered, if not by the inmates' own tears of repentance, then certainly by her own ever-present example of uncomplaining self-sacrifice. When her own maidservants were discovered to be in an unfortunate condition, as inexplicably from time to time happened, the kind patroness of the Magdalens dismissed them from her service, as was consistent with Christian virtue, but was able immediately to experience the joy of placing them in that institution founded with the help of her own money and run according to her own principles where, within a remarkably short time, the majority of the inmates were usually brought to the most abject state of wretchedness and sorrow that the heart of their preceptress could desire.

Such was Madame de Dureville's life, spent in rural retreat in a magnificent château on the banks of the Seine. Not for her the gossip and intrigue, the masked balls and musical suppers, the theatrical entertainments, the merrymaking and luxury that other aristocratic ladies, more profligate and dissolute, professed to enjoy in the company of their husbands and, it must be said, their lovers, in the country as in the capital. Madame de Dureville's repose was rarely disturbed by her neighbours arriving in their carriages to call on her, to invite her to play cards and speculate on each others' love affairs. She had little time to spare for these frivolities, for the butterfly natures which pursued them. Having made it clear that visits from the immoral were unwelcome, she was left undisturbed in chaste seclusion.

She was fondest, in any case, of the society of her inferiors, for these persons could more easily be patronized and condescended to. They were more properly grateful for the services she rendered them. Her equals, she observed, did not always welcome her loving intrusions into their private lives, her willingness to administer sermons and reproofs as though these were infallible remedies like leeches or plasters. The poor, the unhappy, the indigent were generally too depressed, and too respectful to object to this great lady's methods of caring for them, which consisted, in the main, of entering their houses *sans* invitation, commanding them to reveal to her instantly the inmost secrets of their hearts, and scrupling not to enquire of them the most intimate, revealing and shameful details of their physical distress. Whereas the great ladies of the district had several times, in her sad experience, thrown up their hands in horror at this meddling behaviour, it was a rare peasant brave or depraved enough to drive her with oaths and deprecations from his door. No, the poor she could always visit, even if the houses of her acquaintance remained obstinately closed against her.

Madame de Dureville relished hearing of a good misfortune as others might relish eating a good dinner; for it afforded her the opportunity to value all the more her own virtuous estate, uncontaminated by poverty or privation of any sort, her own capacity for generosity in relieving the sufferings of others, and to count the numerous blessings and privileges attendant upon her income and her rank.

For she knew her duty very well. Upright and erect, she carried herself like a true daughter of Sparta, never flinching from even the most painful responsibility, such as evicting tenants for non-payment of their rents, which fell to her lot. Starving peasants, if they died upon her husband's lands, she ordered the parish priest to bury at her own expense, for she heard the grumblings of discontent when harvests failed and taxes rose, and she was determined to stave off, if she could, any pretensions on her tenants' part to feeling *oppressed*, as she heard one fellow in prison put it, or *hard done by*, as his widow subsequently complained.

She did love a deathbed. One of her favourite diversions was attending the dying and their families. Not only was there the expiring victim of accident, tragic mishap, sudden blow or unexpected fatal disease to sustain with prayer and to lead to fear of eternal damnation and final repentance, there was also the exquisite pleasure of the survivors to be questioned, succoured, interfered with, exhorted, comforted and watched. In these cases Madame de Dureville excelled herself. The misfortunes of others drew from her the most excited sympathy, the most ardent willingness to become the sage patroness around whom, because she was privy to each one's secret fears and sorrows, the lives of the mourners might revolve.

When a daughter was born to her, Madame de Dureville accepted this trial without a murmur. Begging her husband's forgiveness for not being able to present him with an heir, asking his indulgence of her need to abstain, for some little time at least, from his embraces, she withdrew to a life of even greater restraint than formerly, handing the child over to a wet-nurse and then retiring to her own apartments to fast and pray in silence.

– God scourges us in His love, her confessor observed to her: not for us to question His wisdom or His ways!

Why her daughter should live when several sons had died stillborn, why she should flourish and grow, developing into a sturdy child who pulled her nurse's hair and laughed and held out her chubby arms to her mother, was a mystery Madame de Dureville did not pretend to understand or to unravel. She contented herself with contemplating it during her prayers. Not for me to call Providence to account! she would say, sighing, as she rose with reddened eyes from her prie-dieu.

During this period of her daughter's infancy and early childhood the good-hearted woman did everything she could to mortify her natural desires and impulses so much inflamed by the recent experience of maternity. She put the little one from her as much as possible. She attempted rarely to caress or indulge her. She caused her never to be allowed treats or indulgences, and the most trifling of gifts, which arrived from distant relatives or friends from time to time, she directed to be given away to the poor. Once she was obliged, upon her confessor's advice, to return to her husband's bed, she obtained permission, at the same time, to abstain from all food, not only from meat, on Fridays, to flay her naked shoulders with the discipline on feast days, and to wear a hair shirt under her hooped brocade skirts.

Madame de Dureville's husband admired her unconditionally for her goodness, and for the sweetness with which she met all the demands made upon her. Though she shrank from the more sensual and depraved embraces to which he liked to subject her in private from time to time, she compelled herself to receive his advances with a manner which perfectly combined compassion with distaste. Monsieur de Dureville counted himself fortunate to have secured her, above all others, for his wife. She was noble as well as beautiful, and she came to him with a large dowry. Best of all, she did not require his constant company. While he absented himself in Paris to dance attendance on the King and Queen, while he travelled about on business or went on hunting expeditions with his friends, he relied upon her never to reproach him for his absences but to continue devoting herself to the care of his bastard children who arrived regularly every nine months after he had paid a visit to his estate, and setting an example to her neighbours of perfect Catholic motherhood.

Monsieur de Dureville often confided in his mistresses that his wife was a martyr destined for heaven. So saying, he protected her from too much knowledge of these wicked women into whose snares he fell with unfortunate regularity, for he wished to cause her no additional grief, and not to add to the burdens she already bore. He kept away from her as much as possible, therefore, dividing his time between the aristocratically bucolic

61

entertainments offered at Versailles and the more elaborate balls and *salons* of Paris, while his mistresses, chosen for their utter dissimilarity to his beloved wife, sought ceaselessly to console him for the separation he endured from his angel. About his daughter he scarcely ever thought, for the very good reason that he never saw her.

Because Madame de Dureville was determined to attempt to love her daughter as a good Christian should, and because she desired for her all the advantages of a superior education such as she herself had enjoyed, and because she did not wish to indulge herself, and simultaneously spoil the child, with the expression and demonstration of too much exquisite maternal feeling, she decided to send her daughter away once the latter reached a convenient age for being parted with, that is to say, on her seventh birthday. She summoned the child from her little room at the other end of the house, and received her in the boudoir where she was wont to spend what few hours of leisure she had in prayer.

The child, who had never entered this room before, looked about her with interest as she rose from her filial curtsey and received permission to sit on a stool at her mother's side. The large crucifix and gloomy religious pictures were not remarkable to her, for a similar style of furnishing prevailed at her end of the house. What gave her pleasure, however, and caused her eyes to sparkle in a most lively manner, was the rich satin of her mother's dress, the elaborate lace of the *fichu* adorning her white shoulders, and the brilliance of the jewels that clasped her neck and arms. For her part, Madame de Dureville surveyed her daughter critically. So far, she had to admit, the girl did her parents credit.

Eugénie (for such was the little one's name) had a graceful carriage and lovely person. Her mind, modelled upon her mother's, was pure as an empty pot, her character pliant and obedient. Schooled in the principles of well-bred reserve and independence, she did not utter a word in the presence of her elders unless these latter first addressed her and encouraged her to speak. She had been taught never to confide in inferiors such as maidservants, but to condemn their pettiness and frivolity. Her confessor had admonished her always to open her heart freely and without scruple to those in authority over her, in order to be sure that the girl had no secrets from him or from her mother. Now, thought Madame de Dureville: the good nuns would complete the process.

– The sisters will teach you courtly manners, etiquette and dancing, she informed her daughter: grammar and handwriting, the more complicated stitches in embroidery, and, I hope, the meaning of Christian renunciation.

She waved her hand imperiously at her daughter.

– Now you may go. Leave me.

Eugénie spent the next ten years locked up behind the high stone walls of the convent of the Sacred Sigh. Her education went exactly as planned. To the feminine accomplishments already adduced above she added, thanks to the ceaseless dedication of the good nuns, a complete conviction of her worthlessness as a sinner before God, and an unshakeable devotion to the mother who occasionally wrote to her. For her father, who did not communicate with her in any way, she entertained the reverence due to a god, freely imagining him to be a heroic personage resplendent with all the virtues and prevented from visiting her only by the exigencies of his calling as one obliged to attend upon Their Royal Majesties.

Having abstained from enjoying their daughter's presence for ten years, the parents duly had their reward once Eugénie quitted the convent which had for long been her home and arrived in her father's mansion in Paris. Her education now being complete, she availed herself of her father's promise, made when she was ten years old, that one day she should visit him in the capital and make her début in the world. And, as though to vindicate his generosity, and good sense, within one month of introducing his lovely and accomplished daughter to the circle of his intimate acquaintance, the father received no fewer than a dozen offers for her hand in marriage.

There was no doubt in Monsieur de Dureville's opinion as to the most eligible of the suitors: Monsieur de Frottecoeur towered above the rest by virtue of the philosophical and scholarly bent of mind that predisposed him to the calm enjoyment of both rural and domestic life. Experienced in the ways of the world, he was old enough to be not merely a companion for

Eugénie but also a guide and mentor. Besides this, he was very rich, and in exchange for the virginal person of his young bride (young, fresh and unsullied virgins being a rare enough commodity in the Paris of those days) was willing to pay off all the father's gambling debts.

– I shall take her to live on my remotest estate, promised the ardent suitor: heaven forbid that such a sweet flower should be contaminated by the foul airs of Paris!

Madame de Dureville, on one of her rare visits to her husband's mansion, was heartily in agreement with her husband as to the suitability of the alliance. She sent for her daughter and informed her of her fate.

Eugénie knelt at her mother's knee, overcome by filial emotion. She kissed the maternal hand extended to her and bathed it in her tears, then, becoming aware of Madame de Dureville's displeasure, tried heroically to check her sobs. Seeing the efforts her daughter made to compose herself, the mother clasped her in her arms in a sudden movement of joy.

– Thank heaven, she declared: we found you a husband so quickly. Now I shan't have to worry about you any more. I only hope you're grateful for all we've done for you!

Eugénie kissed her mother's hand again. She returned to her own room, prostrated herself in front of the crucifix and poured out her heart to her Saviour in silent prayer.

She met her husband-to-be on several occasions before the wedding, and was able to ascertain that, as a man of the world some twenty to thirty years older than she, he was infinitely her superior. To him henceforth she would look up as her mentor, her guide. His hands were fine and very white, his mode of address was ineffably courteous, and his mind was distinguished by a mixture of rigour and delicacy. His learning she could not match, but her manners passed muster with her elderly suitor. On observing her curtsey he patted her cheek, offered her a bonbon, and called her *a sweet child*.

On their third meeting, Monsieur de Frottecoeur condescended so far as to inform Eugénie of the passionate interest with which he was currently pursuing his researches amongst certain ancient philosophical authors of

64

Rome and Greece, and his resolution, as an amateur historian of cultural artefacts, one day to complete his authoritative catalogue of the collection of antiquarian relics formed by his father and added to by himself. This gargantuan labour he had often had to lay aside, because of the pressure of his duties elsewhere, both on his estates and at Paris and Versailles, where he was obliged to dance regular attendance on Queen Marie Antoinette, but now, he promised himself, marriage to Eugénie would provide him with fresh energy for his task.

They were walking in the corridor behind their box at the opera at the time. Rapidly ascertaining that no one was observing them too closely, Monsieur de Frottecoeur went down on one knee, pressed Eugénie's hand to his lips, and assured her of the esteem he entertained for her mind and the desire he felt for her hitherto unravished person.

– In earlier and freer times, my dear Eugénie, he said, smiling: I would have been able to enjoy you without all the bother of having actually to marry you. Since your parents will it, however, I bow to their wisdom! Marry you I must, if I am to benefit from your youth and beauty, and let us hope it will be too onerous for neither of us!

– Oh sir, Eugénie cried: it is too late to draw back now. Do not, I beg you, deprive me of the sweets of this union for which my soul so ardently longs!

To herself she added: do not expose me as a laughing-stock! Oh! Protect me from this disgrace, this humiliation! And above all, protect me from having to return to boarding-school!

Monsieur de Frottecoeur acquiesced to her plea. And so, very early one morning a week later, Eugénie was married to the man of her choice, in the chapel on the main family estate. She was attired as befitted her youth and status, in a simple but costly dress of white muslin, in the shepherdess style made fashionable by the Queen, and she was attended by twenty of the Magdalens and their orphan children, all scattering rose petals.

There were no guests at the ceremony, apart from the Comtesse de Franval, a beautiful and somewhat mysterious widow of mature years who was a close friend of the bridegroom and had promised him to do all she could for his bride and protégée. This task she had undertaken even before the ceremony, entering Eugénie's bedroom just as she had finished dressing and showing her how to secure her wreath of silk lilies at the most becoming angle. She seemed very disappointed that there was nothing else to do for the young bride.

— Oh you little rogue, she cried: you dear sweet rustic girl, how could you dress yourself so fast, all unaided except for your maid? Far better to have summoned my assistance. I assure you, it takes me several hours in the morning before I am ready to go out. A woman's appearance, you know, is a work of art, and must not be rushed.

The chaplain was perhaps the most magnificently dressed of them all. For this nuptial Mass of his favourite penitent's daughter he was clothed in cloth of gold it had taken the local nuns ten years to embroider with pearls and silk thread. So heavy was his cope that he had to be supported to the altar by two young acolytes, upon whose sturdy shoulders he leaned throughout the brief service.

A final canticle was sung by the orphans. Then Eugénie de Frottecoeur, as she was henceforth to be known, emerged, pale and shyly smiling, on her husband's arm.

The wedding breakfast was held, by special invitation of the Mother Superior, in the guest parlour of the convent of the Sacred Sigh. The blushing nuns dropped trembling curtseys to Monsieur de Frottecoeur, whose air of autocratic disdain thrilled them even while they affected not to notice it. His thin fingers were so *very* white! His nose *so* arched and aquiline! His manner *so* curt and abrupt! More than one of the good Sisters took Eugénie aside to remind her of the modest submission that would be required of her from now on. Their anticipation of her delight was met by the bride with a gentle sigh. She bowed her head, pulling her white lace scarf more closely around her throat.

The bridegroom, impatient of the sweet wine and cakes offered by the nuns and seemingly anxious to gather his new wife to his bosom, ordered his horses to be put to and the carriage brought round. Eugénie, mounting into this handsome equipage, was rather surprised to find herself followed by the Comtesse de Franval, whom she had not expected to find one of the party. This lady, imperturbably settling herself, well wrapped in furs, opposite the startled bride, remarked graciously upon the inclement weather and bad roads to be expected on the route southwards, and her hopes of helping to amuse Eugénie on what promised to be a long and tiresome journey.

Since her husband, entering the carriage at that moment, spoke appreciatively of his friend's kindness and forethought towards his new wife, Eugénie forced herself to believe that she shared his sentiments, and that her unease when presented with an unexpected travelling companion arose from no other source than her ignorance of customs obtaining amongst the well-born in *milieux* other than the convent. Her father, she remembered, on being introduced to the Comtesse at the wedding breakfast, had subsequently spoken of her in highly appreciative terms. Where her father approved, she, Eugénie, would not be slow in following. She composed herself with a brief prayer to the Virgin, and smiled timidly at the great lady opposite.

The Comtesse was certainly an object worthy of study. Her slender figure and flowing jet-black hair gave the impression of youthful attraction and seductiveness, even if a closer inspection of her charms suggested that the aid of artifice, in the shape of pads of false hair, bottles of dye, tight lacing, and pots of rouge and of white lead, had been summoned to give her that illusion of freshness which the gentlemen of that epoch required in their female friends. Her teeth, which had all fallen out when she was forty, she had had replaced with shining rows of pearly porcelain. Her apparel was costly and elaborate, for her friends, seeing her distress as an unpensioned widow, grudged her nothing, and responded with alacrity to her most whimsical demands. Monsieur de Frottecoeur, on the occasion of his marriage, had given her a new parure of diamonds, and had promised her she should inherit well under the terms of his will.

Her capacity to attract, thought Eugénie, covertly watching her, was easy to define. She had a high, trilling laugh, a way of pouting and peeping through her eyelashes that was girlishly coquettish; she had a finely turned

67

ankle and the ghost of former beauty. Her prettily accented and haltingly spoken French betrayed her foreign origins; though resident for fifteen years in France she had never learned to converse fluently in any but her native language.

It was her foreignness, decided Eugénie, that constituted her principal attraction: the hint of exoticism in the black eyes and black eyelashes, in the imperious gestures of her little hands with their impossibly long fingernails, the flavour of world-weariness, nay, even decadence, that clung to her languid and muskily scented person. She conveyed a familiarity with arcane and forbidden knowledge. She suggested a certain sensual expertise. She was clearly a mistress of all the arts of seduction.

They were now entering a region of deep and gloomy forest. Inside the well-sprung carriage, however, all was comfort and warmth. While Eugénie discreetly fingered her rosary, hidden in the wide sleeves of her mantle, for she did not wish to upset her husband, who, as she very well knew, was the epitome of worldliness, by appearing too obviously apprehensive of the night to come and the revelations it would afford her girlish innocence, Monsieur de Frottecoeur leaned back in his corner, fingertips together, and discoursed to the Comtesse de Franval of the opposition of Virtue and Vice, a topic of perennial fascination to his philosophical mind.

— There sits Virtue, he exclaimed, waving a hand at his wife, who sat with her eyes cast down and her complexion suffused with adorable blushes: there she trembles, devout and ignorant! But what will she become, I wonder, when confronted by Vice? Is it possible that such purity could be corrupted?

— The true moralist, my friend, remarked the Comtesse: would certainly wish to find out.

She left her seat and placed herself next to Eugénie. Smiling, she threw off the young woman's mantle, and drew the white scarf away from her neck, exposing the flesh of her throat and shoulders. Her fingers brushed back and forth over Eugénie's breast as she rearranged the latter's costume and spoke to her in a voice of caressing contempt.

— See, little one, how pretty you are, and how much prettier you could make yourself if only you would leave off your convent ways, your convent prudery.

The older woman's gentle touches on her shoulders and breasts as she pretended to be solely concerned with rearranging her clothes threw Eugénie into confusion. Against her will she experienced a sensation of inner heat and rapture to which she thrilled as the Comtesse's hands continued to press lightly here and there, deftly and rapidly, on the thin cloth covering her bare flesh.

Monsieur de Frottecoeur smiled as he looked on. Then he came to sit on the other side of his wife, while the Comtesse tore open the front of Eugénie's muslin dress and slid her cool hand inside it.

– You know, don't you, said the husband to his shuddering spouse: that I am your master now. You owe me total and tireless obedience, like that of a slave. Your goods, your clothes, the paltry possessions packed in your trunks piled on top of this carriage, all these things are now mine. More than that, I also possess your person, your soul, your mind.

Eugénie felt she ought not to show dismay: the nuns, after all, had described marriage in similar terms. She raised her lovely face and looked trustfully at her husband. Her lips parted, to emit the faintest of sighs. She thought of her mother, of that lady's beneficent sternness, of the maternal solicitude which unselfishly banished her daughter to the sweet trials of married life in order to strengthen her for life's pilgrimage culminating, who could tell how soon, in death and heaven.

– A woman's education, the Comtesse remarked: is not complete until she has learned truly to look up to her husband as she once did her father and as she would a priest, and if some little chastisement is needed to help her along this way then so much the better! I wonder, my dear Eugénie, whether you are ready to be thus tried?

Staring full into Eugénie's face all the while, she continued caressing her, running her hands lightly over the young woman's breasts until she produced such an effect of heat and of melting that Eugénie panted with excitement, gazing at her husband with apprehension not unmixed with the most delicious fear. He gave her chin a sharp pinch.

– The nuns and your mother have trained you well, little one. You must allow me to add a few refinements of my own.

He tore her lace scarf in two and approached her threateningly with it. She blushed with beautiful shame as he bent over her half-naked body.

– Under your meek manners, mused Monsieur de Frottecoeur: there lurks, perhaps, a wolfish vixen, who scratches and spits. Young girls, I am informed, are the most dangerous animals of all. But I shall tame you, never fear.

With one length of lace he tied Eugénie's hands behind her back, brutally wrenching her delicate wrists as he did so, while with the other Comtesse de Franval gagged her so that she could not cry out. Then they threw her on her back, pulled up her skirt and petticoats, and tore off her underclothes, revealing her private parts, palpitating and scarlet under the effects of the sensual delirium she had just passed through.

Eugénie was astonished by her husband's behaviour, but she did not resist. Good manners forbade it, also the forbearance she owed him as her master. She could not believe that his behaviour was quite normal on such an occasion, but she supposed it must be, for she knew from the nuns that male lust brooked no delay, no refusal, but must be instantly sated if irreparable damage were not to ensue to the swelling organ of supreme male potency. She prepared herself, therefore, for the sacrifice of her virginity, by closing her eyes and silently reciting the Our Father. But this modest refuge was to be denied her. At the touch of the Comtesse's hand on the pulsating core of flesh between her legs her eyes flew open again. Her husband laughed, and slapped her.

– It's for your good that I do this. You understand that, don't you? My beautiful little idiot.

She was reminded instantly of the Mother Superior of her convent school. Her heart almost burst with emotion: never had she expected to find under the flattering love of a husband the strict tenderness of a nun. She gazed at Monsieur de Frottecoeur imploringly. Her look was shameless, beseeching him to hurry. It said: I acquiesce in whatever you must do to me.

70

Monsieur de Frottecoeur immediately retired to the opposite seat of the carriage with the Comtesse de Franval, to whom he proceeded to make the most passionate and violent love while Eugénie, helpless to intervene or to protest, looked on. His gaze locked on hers, he addressed her even as he enjoyed the body of her rival.

— Evil dog, he cried to his wife as he thrust: wild bitch, ravening she-wolf!

Sated and spent, he cradled his mistress in his arms. The Comtesse, her clothes in profligate disarray and her opulent limbs carelessly exposed, laughed with triumphant bliss.

— Virtue is not Virtue until she is tested and tried, Monsieur de Frottecoeur exclaimed: you see, Eugénie, I want no simpering and ignorant miss. I seek a heroine with the courage to endure all the trials I prepare for her!

Eugénic had a moment of illumination. With the eyes of her soul she penetrated her husband's heart and understood the reasons for his strange behaviour. She saw him as he really was, a wild, passionate boy, only too vulnerable to beauty and to the promise of love, led astray by wicked and dissolute women older than he, hopelessly corrupted in his early manhood yet longing always for the understanding he was too proud to ask for, the redemption he despaired of gaining, wretched under his bold and careless exterior, his belief in womanhood bruised, and his early idealism shattered, yet, withal, one faint flicker of hope remaining, that, in his wife, perhaps, he had found his saviour, the angel who would lead him back to happiness.

Eugénie's eyes filled with tears of gratitude. Now, at last, she had found her vocation, and, in that sublime moment, when the clouds of distrust parted and the clear light of inspiration shone forth, revealing her mission and her destiny, her exaltation was such that she could not prevent herself from making muffled sounds of pleasure while uncontrollable shudders racked her entire body.

Her husband leaned across and untied her gag. She smiled seraphically up at the man who had inflicted upon her such sweet, such necessary torture.

71

— You enjoyed watching that, did you? he asked: slut!

He struck her across the mouth with his glove. They finished the journey in silence.

The château where Eugénie was to begin her married life was situated in the heart of a desolate and sparsely populated region of woods and swamps. Its position was so damp and gloomy that few servants could be induced to stay there for long: only an ancient housekeeper, a maid, and a couple of menservants awaited the new chatelaine, a situation perfectly pleasing to the husband, who wished there to be as few witnesses as possible to the torments he intended to inflict upon his innocent wife. On arrival at the forbidding mansion he sent Eugénie straight to her room, coolly remarking that he preferred to remain alone with the Comtesse. The poor young girl, incarcerated in a vast, chilly apartment with no fire and only a single candle to see by, shed a few tears on discovering that no housekeeper attended her, no maid arrived to help her bath and change her clothes. Fortunately, however, the austerities of her life at the convent now proved themselves crucial in aiding her to overcome the emergency of the moment. The rigorous training of her youth was vindicated. She brushed her own hair unaided, though, it must be said, with trembling strokes, and put on a pair of clean stockings.

Eugénie was still young. She had a passionate heart, a soul full of holy affections. Hard as it was for her to subdue the sense of indignation which swelled her bosom whenever she thought of being obliged to tie her own shoe-ribbons herself, yet the natural elasticity of her temperament, the optimism of youth, aided by the precepts of Holy Church which whispered themselves to her night and day, convinced her that it would be right, whatever indignities lay ahead, to pay scrupulous attention to the niceties of social decorum and descend to join her husband and the Comtesse for supper. She was, she confessed to herself, extremely hungry.

Monsieur de Frottecoeur and his smiling friend ate roast beef, cold pheasant, and pigeon tart. Eugénie was served with a basin of pig's blood and a plate of sheep's gristle.

— You'll need to build up some strength, my dear, living out here in the depths of nowhere, observed her spouse as he unfolded his damask napkin: I want to fatten you up a little. A skinny woman is no use to me!

He beckoned to the manservant to pour him a glass of claret.

– I don't like to see women drinking wine, he observed: it's the ruin of them, physically and morally. There's nothing uglier in this world to look at than the face of a woman when she's taken drink.

Eugénie smiled to indicate her agreement, watching the Comtesse languidly emptying her own glass of the ruby-coloured nectar. Swallowing the pig's blood in dainty sips, she reflected that she ought to rejoice at this opportunity, provided so early on in her married life, to mortify herself a little for the sake of sinners, and began to suspect that further chances to practise heroic Christian virtue would not be denied her.

After dinner the Comtesse declared herself in need of the refreshment of slumber, and slipped away. Monsieur de Frottecoeur also seemed fatigued. He yawned, and drummed his fingers on the tablecloth. He complained that he was in need of solitude and repose after the rigours of the journey, and declared that he proposed to repair immediately to the library, a vast apartment on the other side of the house, to commune in peace with the thoughts of some of the great philosophers enshrined in the handsomely bound volumes, the numbers of which ran into many thousands, that lined the library's walls.

– These books he declared: I expressly forbid you to read, Eugénie, lest their perusal should sully the purity of your young mind, which exists, like Paradise before the Fall, in a charming state of perfect nature, innocent of rational thought, untrained in the apprehension of reason, incapable of straying towards the dangers of abstract speculation.

Eugénie bowed her head.

– To men's lot, pronounced the irascible husband: falls the necessity of intellectual and moral action. A woman's grace is that of simply being, without artifice, without striving. Study the roses in the garden, my dear Eugénie, emulate them as simply and quietly as possible, and you will not go far wrong.

Eugénie reflected that these ideas were scarcely new. She had heard

73

them from the nuns many times, those ladies being well equipped with the faculties of exhortation and repetition. Nevertheless, she swiftly banished from her mind the degrading suspicion that her husband might occasionally be guilty of unoriginality, reminding herself that what she might perfectly know in principle, she had yet to endeavour to perfect in practice. She dropped him, therefore, the deepest and stateliest of curtseys and maintained a respectful silence.

— There's a good child, jovially exclaimed Monsieur de Frottecoeur: now be off with you to bed. I have a great deal of reading to do before morning and don't want to be plagued by your whining words and reproachful looks.

Clapping his wife on the shoulder, he led her to the door, pushed her out of it, and unceremoniously shut it upon her.

Eugénie clasped her hands together in anguish. The suffering she endured in that moment threatened her with a violent swoon. She contented herself, however, with a hearty burst of tears. So she was not, after all, to be initiated tonight into those holy hymeneal rites, those most sacred mysteries of the marriage bed. She was not, after all, to be gathered to her husband's heart in the most rapturous of embraces. Her heart was not to be pierced with that agonizingly sweet pain the nuns had hinted at. She groaned aloud.

— It is another, not I, she cried: that he wishes to wound with his sharp arrow of love. Alas, poor Eugénie, now must you taste humiliation. Now must you indeed drain the cup to the bitter dregs.

Slowly she climbed the stairs to her room, vainly attempting to compose herself, pondering, in all the simplicity and naiveté of her girlishly ardent soul, how best to help her husband achieve his unspoken ambition and find true happiness in the married state. Only too conscious of her own inadequacies and shortcomings, which, indeed, her mentors had always been at pains to point out to her, she doubted that it was in her power to do more than struggle to achieve patience. On the other hand, however, the glorious vision would keep on rising up within her, of a grateful husband, hands outstretched and tears of repentance in his eyes, coming towards her to kiss the hem of her gown and beg for her forgiveness. In the achievement of that holy aim she could, she knew, put up with anything.

She gained her room, deciding that before she sought her couch she would write a letter to her mother about all that had happened to her that day. Certain details, she reflected, might have to be omitted, but she had hopes of creating, none the less, a sufficiently fascinating narrative.

Worn out by hunger, exhaustion, excitement, joy, terror, despair, and the awful strain of letter-writing, she hardly remembered getting into bed or falling asleep. The next thing she knew was that a grim-faced maid was pushing open the shutters to reveal the mist of early morning, and informing her, at the same time, that the Comtesse, during her nocturnal ramble in the nearby woods, taken to alleviate the pains of insomnia, had been attacked by a wolf, badly mauled, and had barely escaped with her life.

— What! exclaimed Eugénie, falling back white-faced upon her pillows, her hand going up to cover her mouth: are there wolves in this region?

— Indeed there are, replied the maid: though to be exact, it is better to call them werewolves. Haven't you heard tell of them before now? The country round here is famous for them.

— What, faintly enunciated her tremulous mistress: wild beasts outside the house as well as in it?

Warned by the maid's puzzled look, she recalled her wandering thoughts to their customary shelter of discretion, and lapsed into silence. Some kind of evil dream, she began to remember it now, had disturbed the habitual sweetness of her slumbers. Something dark, and ferocious, and hairy, had interrupted and soiled the peace and purity of her repose. She shuddered at the memory. She wiped her delicate white hand convulsively across her lips, almost fancying she tasted blood.

— My beloved husband, she murmured: I must go to him at once!

The maid declaring in a manner that only too clearly showed how much she relished her insolence, that she was forbidden to wait upon her new mistress or help her in any way, Eugénie dismissed her with no more than a gentle sigh. Pausing only to hurl herself on the floor in front of her

75

crucifix for a brief orison and a hearty burst of tears, she bent her intelligence to the new task confronting her: how to lace up her stays without assistance. Recalling how the fashion for déshabillé, initiated by the Queen, had recently swept the *salons* of Versailles and Paris, she concluded that she could leave aside those articles of apparel indicating the need for lacing, and contented herself with donning the same simple white dress that she had worn the day before.

Simplicity, she reflected, as she gazed at her wan face in the glass, would lend her speed, and speed was surely of the essence if she were to help her husband escape from the traps of sin towards which his dreadful mistress lured him and in which she clearly intended to keep him a prisoner. Busy with these heroic reflections, Eugénie quitted her bedroom an hour later satisfied that her laces and ribbons were tied, her hair was in order, her gloves were fresh, and that she had no need to be distracted by thoughts of beauty or the need to impress. It was on her own courage and virtue, and of course the help of the Most High, that she would henceforth rely. She therefore ran along the corridor as fast as possible and sought the main staircase without delay, the rapidity of her progress increased by her desire to reach the breakfast table before the coffee grew cold.

But alas! She turned the corners too hurriedly, and became hopelessly lost. Her path through a series of glittering apartments seemed always to loop back on itself, to bring her back to her starting point. Once or twice she fancied that animal feet pattered behind her, that mocking laughter sounded from behind a screen, that invisible creatures growled from under the sumptuous coverings of ornate fourposter beds. It was very cold. Servants and staircases alike had vanished.

Fear, and an ardent longing for breakfast, lent Eugénie resolution. She decided to return to her own chamber and seek inspiration by adding a postscript to her letter to her mother. Accordingly she went back down the corridor she was in, turned half a dozen corners, and then began opening one door after another, convinced each time that this must be the room in which she had spent the previous night and dreamed her uneasy dreams.

Nothing had prepared poor Eugénie for the strange sights that now met her eyes. In the first room whose door she opened, she saw, when she peeped through the crack, a great quantity of dead babies suspended from the walls by cruel hooks, the stench of blood and decomposing flesh being so acute that Eugénie banged the door to again with great force. In the second room a row of elderly hags, all dressed in swaddling clothes, lay upon cushions crying for their mamas. In the third room a horde of lean, gaunt-faced women fought each other for chunks of raw meat torn from the naked female corpse lying on a silver platter on the table they all clustered angrily around.

Eugénie backed away, her sense of modesty outraged. She was most relieved when the next door she opened led on to the great stairway she had descended the previous night. Feeling sick and faint with moral indignation and lack of food, she went down it, her only support being shock that the revolting lower classes of the district had not been stopped by the servants of the château from invading their superiors' sacred privacy in this way.

Eugénie found her husband in the library, a vast apartment opposite the dining-room, where, she was distressed and surprised to see, preparations for breakfast were not yet under way, so, though she was sure that her lord and master would not wish her to disturb him in his sanctum, his holy of holies, she could think of no better means of advancing the production of hot rolls, fresh butter and blackcurrant jam, let alone a steaming silver pot of coffee, than by enquiring after the health of the Comtesse, the savage attack upon whom the previous night might be thought to embody a grave enough emergency to warrant such disruption of what she imagined was her husband's normal morning routine, to wit, the perusal of several improving tomes in the interval between rising from his couch and calling his valet so that he might be shaved.

She scrupled not, therefore, quietly to tread across the gleaming parquet and to enquire of her husband how he did.

Monsieur de Frottecoeur rose from the chair by the fire into which he had thrown himself some seconds before. His wig was askew, his brocade gown open to reveal the torn lace ruffles of his shirt, and he staggered a little, overcome by a passion he could not repress, while his bosom heaved with excitement and his eyes glittered with a terrifying light.

Eugénie, seeing the delirium which the sight of her produced, halted, deep blushes suffusing her adorable face.

From the deep pocket of his gown her husband produced a small whip, which he waved at the astonished Eugénie.

— All night long, he cried: I have been engaged in the most diabolical debauch the mind of man can imagine, outstripping even those described so glowingly by the divine Marquis. Oh but now, at the moment of perceiving your still unsullied, fresh, and virginal idiocy, my sweet slut, I am roused to yet more frightful visions of crime and punishment. Come wife, obey my commands once more. Take this instrument of torture, caress it in your little white paws, and let us decide together on what part of your untouched body I shall inflict the first outrage.

Seeing his wife open-mouthed and speechless he smiled.

— Or perhaps, cried he: you would prefer to be the torturer. Oh, Eugénie, fulfiller of my darkest dreams, what rapture!

Sweeping aside his gown Monsieur de Frottecoeur revealed his naked nether parts, where barely healed scars, evidence of recent assaults, were clearly visible upon his plump white buttocks.

— Show me, he exclaimed: your unflinching obedience, owed to me as your master, by pretending that I am your inferior, your despised slave, the very lowest of the low!

Eugénie did not quite like to refuse her husband any request, however outlandish or bizarre, since she wished to welcome all the indignities heaven sent her as a means of purification and advancement in virtue. She was not certain, however, that she was adequate to this new task. She had never handled a whip, having never had a pony or puppy to practise on. With a bursting heart she ejaculated a fervent prayer to heaven for guidance, at the same time involuntarily stepping backwards and, in her haste, knocking over a small table as she did so. A pile of leather-bound volumes fell to the ground. Inspiration, from a divine source, she doubted not, took possession of Eugénie. Seizing one of the fallen tomes, she opened it at random.

– Oh sir, she murmured: let us not be precipitate. Let us consult the wise words, the savoir-faire, the practical knowledge, of one of your cherished authors.

She began, in a surprisingly steady voice considering the vicissitudes through which she had already passed that morning, to read aloud what she wished might turn out to be a tale of God's help in time of trial:

FEDERIGO

N ow that it is all over, and we have received word from Naples that my sister is safely arrived there with Giuditta, I give thanks to God who has preserved us in the midst of such great trials and brought us safely through, as He did the Israelites through the Red Sea, as the Scriptures tell us.

I wrote down the ending of this story (which was for my sister another beginning in a way) when I began this book, because my father commanded me to write it, for his own very good reasons at that time.

I thought, then, I would burn this book afterwards, because it was dangerous to write down my thoughts so freely at a moment when the Fathers of the Most Holy Inquisition were searching out heresy in our very town. But since I have not been able to bring myself to burn this book, as I undoubtedly should, and since I am only too susceptible to the delight that writing words on paper can bring, I shall indulge myself by filling in the beginning of this story. Six months ago, when it ended, I could not write it. My mind was in too much turmoil and everything I wished to write down came out the wrong way round or upside-down. Now I shall make the attempt.

About one year before the Inquisitors decided to come here to Santa Salome and to initiate their proceedings against my sister Bona, I had gone to the house of the Contessa Coniglian in Fiacenza to become part of her household for a while. I should have done this sooner, when I was younger, but my father returned from the war badly wounded and needed me to act as his steward for a time and help my mother in his place. The Contessa, hearing of his wounds got in the battle at Mantua fighting under her husband's generalship, wanted to do some good to our family, because she was one of my godmothers, though she was of much higher rank than my father's family. Her husband was fond of my father, and relied upon him, so it came about that the Contessa said she would be my godmother, at my birth, and remain a friend to us. So when she invited me to live in her house for a while, even though my father still needed me at home, sooner or later I had to go.

The Contessa was very busy because now that peace had come she was having a villa built on her farm in the countryside not very far distant from the city walls, where she hoped to be safe from fresh outbreaks of plague. Her steward and the other servants had to run to and fro to see to everything. The architect came and went, and from time to time we drove out to see what progress the builders were making. She gave me a suit in black velvet, and a new hat and shoes, exactly fitting my estate, not yet a full-grown gentleman nor a relative, but not a servant either. I kept her company, because her husband was not yet returned from Mantua, and her ladies, in her opinion, were too stupid for conversation and good only for praying and embroidery.

I was tall, and very thin, with black hair and a dark complexion. The Contessa showed her affection for me, as her godson, by the names she called me. She called me Barley Sugar, or her dear monkey, or Africa. I was her stick of liquorice, her black imp, her vanilla pod. She awarded me the privilege of carrying her letters in to her in the morning. She slept late, after staying up half the night amusing herself with her ladies, and she liked to have her letters that had come for her the day before read to her while she was still in bed, or making her toilette.

81

Father Sebastiano Bagolan was her secretary. He put the letters on a special tray, a very fine one of blue and green cloisonné enamel, and gave them to me to take to my godmother. The stairway up to her bedroom was all of stone, vaulted overhead. It turned around two landings and so came up to the wooden doors in the stone doorway at the top. Here I knocked and one of the women let me in.

That morning the Contessa called to me, so I went forward. It was dark, because the shutters were still closed, so as not to hurt my godmother's eyes. She had weak sight, which was why she needed someone to read her letters to her. I could not see very well but I walked in, and knocked into the side of a screen. This was set, in a curve, in front of the fire, to make a warm space with some light. I could see that the Contessa was seated on her commode, and felt very ashamed that I saw her. Her thighs were like great white puddings with her yellow gown pulled up over them. She was groaning, to try and do her business, and her face was sweaty, and white as pastry not yet cooked.

She heard the commotion I made as I tried to go, and called to me to stay, and to read her a letter, for diversion. So I stood behind the screen out of her sight, and read her the letter that Father Sebastiano Bagolan had put on top.

I do not know why I have written all this down when it concerns things I should not remember, such as how the Contessa made low noises while she listened to me reading the letter and then cried out with relief when I finished it. She called to the women to wipe her and powder her and to fasten her gown. I came out from behind the screen and brought her her slippers. She liked to have me push them on to her feet. The flesh, fat and white, puffed up out of the slippers like rising bread. She made me look at her while she did these things that decent women, like my mother, do in private. So I have not forgotten her hands, plump as the drawing of starfishes that I used to look at in one of my father's books, and the way that the white fat hung down from her arms like sleeves. Her face, in a halo of fat cheeks and chin, was beautiful. She smelled of geranium powder and orange-flower water. To walk she put her hands on the maids' shoulders for support. She rocked across the room like a great toy that children ride upon.

She had gout, and could walk only a few steps. Three of the menservants, and I helping them, carried her down one flight of stairs in the wicker chair she had had her carpenter construct, with wheels on it, so that she could be pushed about from place to place. This morning she chose to eat her collation on the loggia at the back of the house, from which you could look down on the garden below. This garden, planted with sweet-smelling shrubs and trellises of flowering trees, and laid out with gravel walks in between, was a most lovely place, very refreshing even in the full heat of midday.

In this loggia it was cool, though the sun was well up. The floor was of pink and black marble, brought from Verona, set with pots of orange and lemon trees. The walls and ceiling were painted to make it seem a vine grew there and dangled its curling tendrils, with fat bunches of grapes half-hidden between the leaves. When I first came I opened my eyes very wide at this fresco, so wonderfully well painted that it seemed a real vine grew there, with real fruit. The Contessa laughed at me and called me her rustic Pod and told me to pick a grape off the ceiling if I could.

She was full of such jokes and games. When Father Sebastiano talked to us so earnestly of the need to fear sin and avoid occasions of sin, as he did as often as he could, she would laugh at him too, once he was gone out of the room, and she would call him Holy Watering Can and Slobber Chops and Inky Spit, for he was so enthusiastic in speaking of God's judgements on sinners that spittle flew from his lips during his discourses. But the Contessa esteemed him, for his learning, and she said she liked to have such pretty young men about her as himself and myself. He having auburn curls, she called him Chestnut and Prickle and other such names. She made him dress richly enough to do her credit, as one in her service, and she would not let him cut his hair, whose bright colour she loved.

His hands were smooth-skinned and delicate, as fine and tapering as those of a woman. He held a pen with much grace. He gave me lessons in writing, when he observed how bad at it I was, in forming both my letters and the words to express them. Such little skill as I have I owe entirely to him. Certainly my father thought it a benefit of my time with the Contessa, when I returned to Santa Salome, that at least I had got a little polish in writing if in little else. Much of what I learned during that time is best forgotten now, except that this pen wants to write it and will not let me forget it. However, once I have satisfied this pen that wants to practise writing, and have written down all these disobedient thoughts that jump about in my mind, I shall destroy these pages. It is a relief to complete my story, but it will equally give me peace of mind to burn it later, as I know I must.

Father Sebastiano was fetched to join us on the loggia, and he read out the letter a second time.

Father Giovanni Girotto wrote it. Father Giovanni was the parish priest of the town of Santa Salome, where my family lived, and where I grew up, and he was the chaplain to the nuns of the convent of Santa Salome, where my sister Bona was the Abbess. It was only a very small Abbey that she ruled over, with some twenty or so nuns living in it, but the Contessa, when she helped to found it, said that it must be an Abbey. I believe she thought an Abbey would do her more honour, as its patroness, than merely an ordinary house of nuns or even a priory. The Bishop, who wrote the nuns' Rule, agreed with her, and so the house was an Abbey and my sister an Abbess, even though the nuns' church was so small as always to be called their chapel.

They were enclosed, with their strict Rule forbidding them to go out, and their chief employment was praying for the souls of the mother and father of the Contessa. These two persons left the money for the convent, stipulating only that day and night ten of the nuns, at the very least, should be beseeching God on their behalf with their prayers to take their souls out of Purgatory and bring them into Heaven.

Since this praying took up so much of the nuns' time the Contessa had made a very handsome settlement on the convent, so that they wanted for little, and with alms, and a portion of tithes from the villagers, and their own produce which they grew, they could be self-sufficient. And after a while they started selling bread and cakes to the people roundabout, to increase their income. Also they had an orchard, and a vegetable plot, and a fish pond.

The Contessa made Bona the Abbess, for she liked to do good to our family if she could, as I said before, and Bona was of the right age to be a nun, although she said she did not want to become one. But it cost less than getting her a proper dowry, so she consented. She said she did not mind so much since Giuditta's parents were also placing their daughter there.

The trouble with this writing is that it requires such a length of time and so many words to say even the simplest thing. The most difficult part lies in not knowing in what order to put events. It is not obvious to me how to arrange them. My pen skips off now this way and now that, like a child at a fair running hither and thither after all the toys and sweets he wants, or like a lover tempted now to this and now to that by the wanton glances of many mistresses. But I must not talk more of wantonness, though that is precisely one of the sins of which my sister Bona was accused by Father Giovanni in this letter he sent to the Contessa which first I and then Father Sebastiano read to her. I will not write down here again all that he said, since I have written it already in my account of the Inquiry to which Bona and Giuditta were subjected by the Holy Fathers of the Inquisition. I will condense his letter, which was very protesting, and very long.

Father Giovanni accused Bona of practising black arts, and of lewd activities with the other nuns in which she played the man's part, and of shutting the convent so completely against all comers, even himself, that none could go in to find out the truth or otherwise of the rumours current in the village.

People said that Bona performed abominable rites on human children, afterwards tossing their butchered bodies into the street outside the convent wall, and on men and women, tearing off their private parts and then sending them to wander, naked and bleeding, in the piazza. One woman carried her torn-off breasts in her hands, and another clasped her tongue which had been cut off, while the babies were mangled together in an old laundry basket, their necks broken or their throats cut. One dead child had no hands but stumps, which had been gnawed by human teeth. Lastly, Bona had taken the reliquary containing the relics of Santa Salome, given to the convent at its foundation by the Contessa, out of their place in the chapel and had secreted them in her own cell, to use them in some occult practice. The reliquary was shaped like a monstrance, with flaming rays of gold in the form of a burning bush, the gold all encrusted with gems, very beautiful and costly.

The relics were the thighbones of Santa Salome, her breasts and hands and toes, all mostly ground to powder and reduced very small. They had been brought from the Holy Land, whither she had gone on pilgrimage, but where she had been captured by Infidels. When she escaped and returned to her native land, the Emperor Charlemagne told her to wander no more, preaching and doing miracles. But she got as far as our little town, which is named after her, and had the church built, which is very ancient, and then returned to the Holy Land and died there.

The merchant who brought her bones back, led to them by a vision in a dream, sold them to the Contessa, and she had the reliquary made. It was by a miracle that the Contessa got the relics just when she needed them to mark her foundation of the convent dedicated to Santa Salome, for putting them in the convent signified that the prayers said in the chapel where they were kept would be most efficacious, and that therefore the souls of the mother and father of the Contessa would soon be released from Purgatory, with such devoted and holy nuns praying for them in that sacred place. Also they could store up grace for the Contessa herself, asking Santa Salome to intercede for her when she was dead so that her soul would go straight to Paradise.

On hearing the letter read aloud this second time the Contessa coughed very loud and lost half her breakfast on to the floor. Father Sebastiano said it would be a matter for the Inquisition, who would certainly be able to discover the truth of what was happening. I felt very ashamed, for my sister and my family and myself, and wanted very much to go to them as soon as possible, to comfort them and be comforted. I burst out crying, and begged the Contessa to let me go home. Yet I think if she had forbidden me to leave her, I might have felt some kind of relief, that I might therefore be able to avoid this trouble that fell upon us like the foundations of a house giving way and the roof caving in. At any rate she told me to be quiet.

Father Sebastiano read her the second letter. This was from the Bishop of the province of Grezzano, of which the Contessa's house marked one extremity and Santa Salome the other. He wrote merely to ask the Contessa to attend the ceremonial Mass, to give thanks for the victorious peace achieved after so many years of war, which he would offer at the start of Advent, which would be attended by all the great families from the province and be a most splendid occasion. If the Contessa, known to be such a great patroness of the Church Militant, could send him a gift to help him beautify even further the cathedral of Grezzano for this holy occasion, then he would be very grateful to her.

Because the Contessa wore a wide-brimmed hat, with a veil of black muslin hung over the front, to protect her eyes from the sun and to keep the flies away while she ate, I could tell nothing from her face. The veil shook from side to side as she went on eating. While she made her decision I stared very hard at the gilded basket of pastries in front of her, the fluted beaker in red and gold striped Venetian glass, very fine. I stared at them so hard that I remember them very clearly.

The Contessa said she wished to give the reliquary containing the remains of Santa Salome to the Bishop, on the occasion of the Mass to celebrate the end of war. She had no money to buy anything else, since the villa she was having built was costing her so much, and, besides, the relics were the most fitting gift she could think of to mark such a holy celebration.

She said Father Sebastiano would have to go and fetch them, and that I should accompany him, and leave him at the convent doors and return to my father's house. She said that once the relics were removed from Bona's keeping she would lose all her authority, and would have to submit to questioning.

Father Sebastiano said that Father Giovanni said that Bona had shut the convent doors against him and would not let him in.

87

The Contessa replied that Bona, if she were so fond of the company of women as Father Giovanni's letter implied, would certainly not be able to resist that of a young, beautiful and ardent widow seeking asylum and asking to enter the house as a nun. The Contessa said that this lady would be modestly dressed, as befitted one travelling on the annual pilgrimage to Rome, which left Trento very soon and passed near to Santa Salome, and would wear a veil over her beautiful auburn hair. Her companion would carry a parasol, hung with muslin for greater protection and privacy, to shade them both. At night they would make sure to sleep apart from the rabble of pilgrims, in case they were remarked in any way, and as soon as they reached the district of Santa Salome they would depart very discreetly from the pilgrimage, by night if possible, and go into the village.

The Contessa said she was tired of talking so much. She desired Father Sebastiano to go and see to the architect, who had been waiting downstairs for some time, only she had forgotten he was coming again today. She desired me to fetch a book, and read more to her of the romance she had begun to read the day before, set in winter in the snow, and so I did:

ROSA

It snowed even more than usual, that winter our mother disappeared. People dug out their skis, their ice-skates, to help them glide like birds across fields, down the river. In our family we had a big sledge that hung all year in the shed at the side of the house. In autumn my father would take it down, clean and grease it. To be ready for the bad weather, the roads coated in black ice that made you fall down and crack your bones, paths in and out of the village blocked up with snow. This way my father could still fetch supplies. We had potatoes and onions stored in the cellar, plums and cherries preserved in jars, but he had to bring back flour and oil and salt, things like that. Coarse salt, which was for cooking of course, but also to scatter outside round the house to melt the ice a bit. That way you could go out and not slip so much.

My mother vanished in the middle of that winter. It was special, for the amount of snow, and because she went away. We couldn't see what direction she ran in. A fresh fall of snow, and her footprints were blotted out. Funny thing to do, walk out in a snowstorm. But maybe, we thought, she stole some skis or skates and went off that way. Or she hitched a lift from someone taking a sledge into town. No one knew. She disappeared, that was it.

That was the time I first saw the angel. I was thirteen years old. It was the middle of the night. Somehow I don't think you could see an angel in daylight. I found they showed up only in darkness. That was my experience anyway. Perhaps someone really sharp-eyed could see the brightness of the angel against the brightness of sunshine and separate the one from the other. But not me. Also, I think the reason I saw the angel at night was because it was the peaceful time, when I could be alone.

I liked to creep out of our house at night, go to stand in the long grass of the meadow across the lane. Smell it. The cold greenness of the firs that grew all over the countryside, animals and manure, and the sweet scent of the pine trees in the forest on the hill behind the house. Blackness pressed round and you smelled it and you smelled water and mud too. An adventure, that's all. Standing in my nightdress, the kitchen hearth-rug wrapped round me, staring upwards at the sky full of stars. I stood very still so as to disturb nothing, let the farmer's dog go on sleeping, but hear the tiny things, dockleaves swallowing dew, one leaf on the cherry tree slapping another. Hoot of the owls. Often one small animal being killed by another, a scream in the night to signal an invisible death.

Sometimes I went for walks at night right down the lane and towards the village, all around the district. First because I liked it, also because I was looking for my mother, couldn't imagine where she'd got to. Sometimes at night when I woke with a bad dream, she wasn't there. Her place in bed beside my father, in the big bed down the end of the room, empty. My father asleep and snoring, my mother gone. So I'd go out to search for her. In the morning she was always home again, calling to us to get up. Yet I was sure I didn't dream the things I saw at night, they were so real. Certainly my mother said I did. You're the crazy one, she told me: bad girl to make up such stories.

I'd wait at the garden gate until I could see a bit, then let my feet feel their way. Stepping into puddles of blackness, walking on black water. The hedge alongside was a long black blur, kept me going straight. Bare feet in boots crept through the cart-ruts in the mud.

The farmer my father worked for owned all the fields round our house, some of the pine forest at the back, our meadow and orchard too. I kept to the edges of the ploughed and planted land, paced out the space of the field. Forwards then sideways, while my mind jumped about wherever it wanted to go. Then I could know what I thought. Our house was a busy place, full of people and noise and work to get done. After a walk in the fields at night I slept well, brain clear, problems and worries thrown up into the air over the sleeping rows of cabbages and so gone.

Seven of us. Mother and father and five daughters. The eldest: me. Quite normal, being so many. One family on a farm outside the village going the other way, there were fourteen to start with, then some died and that shook it down a bit. Five children were manageable, just about.

Like being in the army, I suppose. Mornings, we lined up just inside the kitchen door, to be checked. Clothes on the right way, clean underwear, shoes polished, hair brushed. My mother was strict about those things. It was called self-respect, and kept you one step ahead of those enemies mud and dust. Just. All day she chased them with brooms and mops, to keep them out. We got to school tidy and clean, were praised for this by the teacher. We set a good example. Our family was good. Parents careful. My mother fed us, my father made sure we each had a pair of rubber shoes to wear for school. In winter we carried them in little linen bags embroidered with our names, put on boots to plough down the lane, the long white drift of snow deep between the hedges, a trough of white. In summer we wore clogs, but often went barefoot for the pleasure of it, put the shoes on just outside the school door.

In the afternoons we worked, those old enough. My task was to mind the younger ones, keep track more or less, see that no one fell into the pond and drowned or cut themselves open on the scythe or ate poisonous berries or weeds. At night we slept in the attic bedroom above the kitchen. Mother and Father at the end near the stairs, with a curtain pinned round them, and us girls down the other end. Two to a bed except for me. I was too restless, they said, I tossed about, groaned and kicked. So I was put in a bed by myself. Being the odd one didn't worry me. Easier to creep out and go downstairs. I found that the midnight walks helped me to calm down.

Seeing the angel was part of this life, not broken off from it. The life at night was secret, but only because the others were asleep. Though I didn't want to be stopped from going out. They might have tried to stop me, my parents, if they knew. So I ended up not telling them. I kept it to myself.

In any case we didn't talk much to each other in our house. There was no talking, but there was looking. I always knew how my mother felt just by looking at her, her expression. She was like the weather. How she felt meant how your day would go more or less.

In those days, however much you loved someone, didn't mean you talked to them. For a start, we were so many. Second thing, terribly busy. Take my mother's life. Often woken in the night by the two smallest ones, then up early to get my father's breakfast, clean the stoves, fetch kindling from the shed, start the fires, get us up and wash and dress us, make our breakfast, get us off to school. In the winter, this is done in the dark and the freezing cold. It's hard to be kind when you feel so cold. My mother tried to keep that one room where we all lived as clean as she could. Mud walked in and out all day on the soles of boots. She laid down strips of cardboard, tracks across that we mustn't stray off. Also she saw to our few animals, grew our vegetables, helped the farmer's wife with her washing.

All day she watched the fire in the tall stove, to make sure it didn't go out, and the fire in the hearth, where she cooked. When the wind was wrong, the chimney smoked, and dropped sticky black soot. We loved the ash in the hearth, wood ash so fine and light like grey snow. We put our hands on it, then on each other, made a fine mess. My father couldn't help my mother much. He worked for the farmer as a labourer, his time was owned by the farmer, that was that. Sometimes late at night my parents whispered to each other about their lives. I heard them clearly though they didn't speak. The silent words of my parents reached me like smells, like the creaking of their bed. In our family what you didn't say was part of the general noise.

If we children fought each other or cried too much or left clothes on the floor, it gave our mother distress. She could manage only if we were well organized, obedient, tidy, good. One child crying, all right, could be muffled by the quiet of the others, but when we all cried and fought it made her suffer. Something broke in her and she got frightened, as though the ceiling fell down or floods came and overwhelmed the house. I felt this in her, sort of a stomach-pain. So, each one, we learned to be good. Not to crack our mother's heart, make her exhausted and unhappy.

It was like breaking in an animal. Training a dog, from wild puppy, biting and making messes, into obedient guardian. One by one we submitted to the rule of our childhoods, gave up the battles, learned self-control. Most of the time. I understood that parents had to win. Their lives were impossible otherwise. Children's wills had to be broken, like twigs. Broken enough so that they could be bent into the parents' design. We five daughters got plaited together, the handle on a basket of hope and faith.

We were ordinary. Exactly like millions of others. That is the way things were. No point complaining. We were poor, always struggling, uncertain. Yet when you're a child you forget family hardships for hours at a time. You run off and play truant, you swim in the river or climb trees, you lie on your back in the long grass and dream, you escape for a little while from the sorrows and the worries about money. Of course my childhood had many happy times. Always outside. That's where I was free.

That year the snow began in early December. One afternoon, when the sky outside the window was grey and heavy. Thick flakes, ragged, dropped softly and silently, blotted out the garden.

My mother stood in the middle of the kitchen, clutching an apronful of potatoes she'd brought in from the cellar. She turned her head from side to side. She made a remark to no one in particular.

— I shan't be able to get to church for vespers if this goes on.

My father came in, stamped snow from his feet on to the mat. Little ice-prints of the soles of his boots fell off.

— Good thing, he grunted: this snow will stop you gadding about.

My mother was the pious one. Most evenings, if she could, she slipped out before supper. Down to the church in the village with its silvery onion dome, to say the rosary, attend vespers. She'd come back flushed, a bit of a sparkle clinging to her like a trail from fireworks. You'd see, then, how pretty she really was when she wasn't always tired. Green eyes that slanted under black eyebrows, black hair held up in combs on top of her head, a generous mouth. Half an hour back in the house, and she was dimmed. Her mouth set, not speaking to anyone, furiously scrubbing potatoes in the sink.

That night I couldn't sleep. The light snowfall outside beckoned to me to come and see it. Urgent as a hand rattling the latch, knocking at the loose panes of the kitchen window. I was glad to go, because my sisters' dreams were thick in the room, colliding with each other, crash, then dissolving into one another like steam. I didn't want to listen to the clatter of their dreams falling in and out of step like altar boys tumbling down the sanctuary steps in church. I didn't want to listen to my father's snores. I hoped my mother wasn't awake and wouldn't hear me creep by. She lay very still. A long mound of quilt, hazy behind the thin curtain.

I put on socks and boots, my mother's overcoat, which covered my nightclothes and just skimmed my toes. The snow was a white sheen, very frosty. It crackled underfoot. A thin crust of it, like stiff white sheets flung down on the ground. I looked at it from the steps down into the garden from the front path, then went on into the meadow.

At first it was peaceful, the snow like a hand over the world's mouth, hushing it, stopping its breath. Then suddenly a wind sprang up. It waved the branches of the trees to and fro, I heard them. The snow creaked and rustled and fell off. It plopped gently on to the snow underneath.

If you were inside the house, looking out of the window, and saw the branches tossed by the wind but could not hear them, it might be very frightening. But here outside I could be part of it and that was not frightening at all.

Then the clouds fled. The wind drove them away. Out sprang the moon. A stream of light whitened the orchard. I saw clearly. I couldn't have been making a mistake. The moonlight was too bright.

The angel was silver. Seemed cut out of solid moon. Hands clasped in front of her waist, she drove herself across the sky. Her wings flew behind her. They flapped to and fro. She passed across the heavens. Just wearing a skirt. Two little breasts that stuck out like silver apples. She smiled but she didn't look at me. She travelled past, steady on her course, like a boat with a propeller. Dark-blue clouds returned and swung shut, closed round her like a curtain.

Bliss inside me, like a feast eaten in secret. So sweet it hurt. I crossed my arms to keep the feeling in. It leaked away, ran out of my arms, between my fingers. The meadow was exactly the same as usual, the compost heap at one end, but it was empty. The moonlight went thin and pale as clouds crept back across.

In the morning I couldn't wake, too deeply asleep to hear my mother's call. She shook me, hands on my shoulders, she pulled me from silvery darkness into the living world. I began crying, then when she shouted at me I cried more.

A day that starts like that, badly, stumbles along in the same way. All of us were late for school, because I'd forgotten to get the boots ready the night before. The others played snowballs going down the lane, it felt too mean to stop them. So we were late. Coming back at midday, the same thing. When we got home my mother wouldn't speak to us because she was tired out, with a headache. The little ones misbehaved, I had to shout at them, then they cried. I was supposed to keep them quiet while my mother got the food ready, but I was half in a dream, and the children were cold and hungry, quick to fight and cry.

In the middle of all this my mother threw the frying-pan on the floor and rushed outside, into the snow. She screamed that she was leaving, how sorry she was we were born, she would kill herself, she would never come back.

The little ones cried louder. We older ones were silent. We knew she meant it. She was gone and she would not come back. Fear inside me said: we will all die.

I told myself she would return. She always had done, so far. But we never knew for sure. We could not believe her, that she really was leaving us. This was the roof going off the house, the walls collapsing. But we could not trust her, either, that she would come back and be our mother again. I felt my stomach was very large, emptied by her going, then blown out with fear. I wanted to eat, to fill myself with her. When she ran out, crying she would never come back, my stomach jumped after her. I ran to the sink in the corner and was sick.

I was the eldest, but I didn't know what to do. I couldn't depend on the air around me. I thought it might give way. It was rough, like a brush, and scratched my face. Crying would do me no good. It made no difference, only made grown-ups angry and hit you. It was too frightening to cry for long, it made you fly into broken pieces, an explosion like windows breaking, then afterwards you felt dangerous, as though you should be thrown away. So I hit the little ones, one by one, to stop them crying, I shouted at them to frighten them so much they wouldn't cry. After I slapped them I pushed them on to their chairs at the table, then I served them the food that hadn't landed on the floor.

My father came home, usual time, sat in his chair by the fire, normal. If it was as usual, my mother was down at the church, saying the rosary. But she didn't come back that night. My father looked as though someone struck him over the head. He stayed in his chair, didn't move. I made supper. Potato fritters and roast onions. Same as yesterday. I couldn't think of anything else. If it was yesterday my mother would still be here. But she wasn't.

When I went out to the cellar to fetch the stuff, I found we were down to our last tray of onions, last few potatoes in the sack.

Snow was falling outside the window. We all watched as my father drew the curtain back, lit the lantern, hung it from the curtain rod. So my mother would see it if she came home. She would know how welcome she was, how much we wanted her. I knew this was what he meant. He didn't need to say it in words. He didn't want to start crying either.

Apart from the lantern, it was an ordinary night. December, snow falling as it did every year at this time.

I said to my father: tomorrow I'll take the sledge down into the village to buy food.

He had a startled look on his face, as though he'd realized just this minute my mother had gone.

— Can't do that, he said: tomorrow we'll be snowed in. We'll have to wait and see.

I leaned against his chair.

— Don't worry, I said: you've still got me. I'll take care of the house. I'll look after the other children. Everything will be all right.

He didn't reply. So I went up to bed.

The staircase was a ladder hidden in a cupboard. With my hand on the door I looked back. My father had his hands stretched to the heat of the fire, that was sunk down and red. He was staring at his hands as though he didn't know what they were.

Once I fell asleep I realized my mother had lost her voice. She'd left it behind in the house when she ran away. Words called by my mother drifted past me like smoke.

Don't touch me no no no go away get your hands off no no no.

In the morning the bedroom was brilliant with white light. I jumped up while the others were fast asleep and it was still calm. My breath melted the ice on the windowpane until I could see out. The world was gone, under heavy snow. Just the top of the hedges showed as blurs of white, the tips of reeds marked the edges of the pond, frozen over and white as the moon. Every tree had a thick white shadow exactly fitted on top of it. The dog's kennel had a white roof of felt. White lumps were the bushes in the garden. White lines drew the gate, the fence.

Too much snow for us to get to the village. I had the idea, too late, of looking for my mother's footprints of yesterday, to see which way she'd gone. But they were filled in by the snow, smoothed out. The snow was like forgetting. It dulled you and slowed you down. It dazzled your eyes so you covered them and couldn't see.

The little ones built a snowman in the meadow. I watched them, then I watched my father dig a path round the house. He unlocked the shed and went in. Then he came out, locked the door again behind him. The keys tossed themselves up and down on the open palm of his hand. Then jumped into his pocket. I wondered if he would hang them back where they usually went, on the nail behind the kitchen door. Somehow I thought he might not.

He saw me watching him.

— Everything in there's frozen solid, he called: the sledge, the lot. I don't want you trying to get the sledge out.

I followed him indoors. He sat by the fire, put out his toe, pushed a heap of grey embers. I kept one eye on him, the other on the last of the potatoes and onions I was peeling for dinner at noon. Dumplings of flour and potato in thin onion broth. With luck stretched to make supper too. Then tomorrow we would have to get down to the village. Somehow or other we would do it.

My father's hands flew about his head. They clenched into fists. They knuckled his forehead, then his eyes. They leaped out of his pockets when he tried to jam them in. The key to the shed fell tinkling to the floor. His hands wrestled with each other in the air. He leaned down and pocketed the keys.

He got up.

— I'll go and put more salt down outside, before it freezes again. Who's coming to help me?

The little ones had finished their small portions of soup. They clustered around him, shouting. He swept them off through the back door.

My mother wasn't coming back. It was time to sort out her clothes. I went upstairs, to the chest that stood beside her bed, and opened it.

Quite a collection she had left behind. Green woollen jacket embroidered with blanket stitch, full black skirt with patch pockets, blue serge blouse with mother-of-pearl buttons. Shawl, petticoats, chemises, drawers. Stockings, mittens, her fur-lined boots. Her winter nightgown of cream-coloured flannel with crocheted lace.

I folded these things up, tucked them below the spare pillows at the bottom of the blanket box. With a piece of scented soap to keep the moths away. Except the nightgown. I kept that out. Too warm and pretty to waste.

Next I went through my mother's jewellery. Her treasure. It was all here. Her wedding earrings of enamel anemones on hoops, her silver First Communion bracelet, her gilt crucifix she wore round her neck on Sundays, a black ribbon pushed through the loop. I tied them up in a red handkerchief I found in her chest of drawers and put them with the clothes. I wanted to take the earrings to wear but it was a bit soon. Better to wait.

I heard the little ones come back in laughing from their game of throwing down salt in the dark. Over-excited. I had to smack them into bed. They were supposed to be good and obedient, but they'd forgotten how. In just two days. To them snow still meant holidays, it stopped them thinking about our mother, where she'd gone. They were just so happy to miss school.

I was still hungry after our small supper. Hunger was a knife whittling my bones. My stomach sucked itself in. I put on the cream-coloured flannel nightgown. I clambered into my parents' bed and laid my head on my mother's pillow. Waiting for my father to come upstairs, I heard the angel come in. A rustle of wings, stiff feathers brushing against glass. She must have unfastened the catch somehow, for there she was, at the far end of the room, leaning into the children's beds, counting heads on pillows, as she searched for me. I lay still and watched her approach. She steered well, with sharp turns round the bedposts, then a nose-dive when she spotted me. She stood on the chest of drawers. It was lit up by her glowing presence, like a silver bonfire with her inside it.

– Never get married, she said to me: never be a wife and mother, never have children.

– I agree with that, I replied: too much trouble and sorrow, children are. They bring suffering, that's all. I'm going to stay with my father and look after him.

Often I'd heard my father complain at my mother. They quarrelled often. It was so terrible to listen to that I always tried to stop them, to calm them down. I would start talking, or go to hug them, or ask a question. But then they would blame each other for upsetting me, and have another fight. So in the end I tried to keep out of their way, not to listen, to block

99

my ears. The one good thing about my mother leaving us was that she and my father could not fight.

The angel waved a wing-tip to make me attend to her.

— What you have to do with children, she told me: is ignore them. If you do that for long enough they stop crying. Then you don't have to smack them and feel so terrible.

She flew low across the floor like a big silvery moth. She darted out of the window, closing it after her with a flick of one wing.

When I woke up in the middle of the night my father was tucked in next to me. He hadn't tried to wake me, move me back to my own bed. In his sleep he moaned and wept. I touched his cheek.

— Don't worry, I whispered: I'm here.

Then I thought: but what if he decides to marry me?

In the morning I heard the clatter of the fire being raked out downstairs. Hunger pierced me, and the cold white light in the room from snow fresh fallen. I put my head into the hollow my father's head left in the pillow. Smoothed by his cheek, smelling of him. I said a prayer to it, to blot out my dream. The butcher's shop in the village where warm blood soaked into the sawdust and attracted flies. Thick flesh of carcasses, a bright red, ribbed with thick white fat the butcher prised off like a white jacket. My mother dangled from a steel hook in the corner. The priest was saying a Requiem Mass on the butcher's block while my father kicked at a litter of sawn bones.

He was whistling when I went downstairs. I tiptoed on stockinged feet, wanting the little ones to stay asleep. As soon as they woke they'd begin crying for breakfast. I had to find something to give them.

— Snowed in again, my father said.

He spat on his hands, rubbed his palms together. He pulled and heaved on the front door, which swelled with the wet, and stuck. He shoved and grunted. Inch by inch it opened. Then it yielded and gave way. He leaned a hand on the porch wall. He panted, red-faced.

— Fetch me the shovel, Rosy Posy. Hurry up.

I found it by the back door and took it to him. I stood and watched his back strain and bend, his arms lift snow and chuck it to one side. Winter would mean repeating this labour every day. Winter was an icy field stretching far off, with no track through it, in which only hunger grew. Round the house, out the back, was the vegetable plot. A few potatoes and turnips might remain there, frozen, deep down in the rocklike earth. I could try to hack them out. But I was too sleepy, too hungry. I felt weak. All I wanted was to go back to bed and pretend we were all fine, no problems.

Once I saw our cat worry a dead bird after killing it. Rip into its flesh with needle claws, blunt muzzle coated with blood. Hunger attacked my stomach like that. Also hunger was gassy, blew me out like a balloon.

When I went back inside the kitchen pushed at me like a person, saying get out of here. It was chill and empty without my mother's stooped back, at the sink or the stove, her thin shoulders under the crisscross straps of her flowered overall. A wine bottle lolled on its side near the fireplace. The floor needed sweeping. The tablecloth was crusted with dried bits of food the children dropped last night at supper.

I got myself out of that sorrowful room. I hated whoever it was telling me to go, that she hated me for what I'd done, that I could never be forgiven. A small, ill-wishing voice that hid in the chimney. I shut the front door behind me, hoping I left all the sorrow behind me, closed up, to starve to death.

Standing in the porch I shivered. My father had dug a narrow path between banks of snow, in the shadow of the one he dug yesterday. It curved around the side of the house. Gritty under my feet when I stood on it. Having to put salt down fresh every day, soon we'd run out.

The path didn't stop at the shed. My father had dug further. His tunnel track went across the garden, plunged into the meadow. I understood. He was trying to reach the back road that ran into the village, since the snow in our lane was too deep to get through. He would return. Then he and I would take the sledge and go into the village and buy food.

I knew this wasn't true. My father had left too. It was clear to me he'd gone off looking for my mother. He loved her. He had to pursue her, to find her and bring her back. He couldn't wait for her to return of her own choice. She tugged him after her like a sledge skimming the snow. Whistling over packed ice. He glided on sharp runners, he sped over the frozen fields. He would draw her back to him, swiftly, over the gleaming snow.

I wasn't beautiful like my mother. Two skinny black plaits, small black eyes, a button nose and mouth. Nothing special in the way of looks. She was the one with the force to make men notice her. The way she turned her head, spoke, moved. She pulled their eyes. My mother was the queen. It was simple. We were children, bodies she pushed and washed and fed. For my father she kept the glints, the swing of hair, the tone of voice. But for my father I was special too. He always said to me, before all this happened: don't throw yourself away on some good-for-nothing farm boy. Plenty of time. Don't you love your old dad?

I stood on the path of trampled snow and shivered. In my skirt pocket my fingers curled round the shed keys which I'd lifted from under my father's pillow this morning. He'd forgotten them there. He'd forgotten he needed to keep them safe. How I put it to myself was: I'll just go and check in the shed. Just to make sure there aren't any supplies I've over-looked. And if there's nothing, then I'll take the sledge, and all the children, and try to get down to the village. Of course it will be all right.

It was a task I set myself. One: get into the shed. Two: search for food supplies my father's forgotten about. This could fill ten minutes, get me through that small bit of time, make me think of something else beyond being so hungry, my skin prickled to bumps, my heart knocking about.

The door swung open. Quite normal. Dark in there, floor clammy with cold through the soles of my boots. Cold congealed in the corners. Laid itself on my face like a rough hand.

The sledge was in its usual place, parked along the far wall. Under the tiny window smeared with cobwebs and dirt. Frost had put a pattern on the square of glass, delicate ferns. Icicles dipped down, thick tips of ice melt-ing at their points, like broken bars.

How could my father have forgotten? How could he not have told me that we had so much food stored away in here?

The long bundle on the sledge was covered by a tarpaulin shining glossy grey.

102

Then I remembered. He'd said it was all frozen solid in here, that the sledge was unusable.

On top of the tarpaulin there was indeed a coat of ice. Stiff to my fingertips when I prodded it. A coffin of cold, that kept the food inside it perfect, fresh. It could not decay. My hands couldn't loosen the tarpaulin. It was grafted by ice on to the bundles of food below, close as a skin. I struck my hand angrily against it, bruised my knuckles. Beads of blood sprouted on the bruised flesh.

I had no control over my knees. Hunger undid me, my muscles, my balance. I dropped down. I couldn't stand up any longer. I crouched next to the sledge and studied it. Food. Out of reach. Do not touch me no no no.

I was starving, I was alone. Abandoned in a desert of snow. Cut off from everybody. The ice sang to me, it was triumphant and cruel. Lie down and die. Lie down and die.

Last night, in the middle of the darkest hours, in the core of night, I'd woken to discover my father's face an inch from mine. I smelled his sour-sweet breath and heard his flickering snores. I listened to the words that floated past the end of the bed like homeless ghosts.

My fault my mother is gone.

I'm so hungry I could die.

I'm so wicked, I made her go.

I huddled on the floor of the shed and shivered. I was so afraid that I couldn't get up. If I stayed very still then whatever it was might not notice me.

A shift of light in the doorway. The angel's shadow, crisp gold. So she did appear in the daytime after all. Seemed queer to me. The sun was behind her, I couldn't see her face. Just her arm upraised, her long forefinger pointing.

– Listen, the angel said: your mother is in Paradise, and I have come to tell you how to get there:

CHERUBINA

My country is called Paradise. It is little known. Most people believe it might have existed once but are certain it is now lost for ever. They say only madmen go there, some poets. To that vanished place; ruined; its broken columns covered by drifts of desert sand.

Yet some adventurers spend their lives trying to discover it. Archaeologists searching for buried cities, in the deepest heart of the world, or under the sea. Explorers convinced there is one unknown valley hidden in the high mountains that they haven't yet reached. For some my country might turn up in the fragments of broken pottery they unearth from a cache in a scrubby wilderness. For others it might be traced in the secret language women use for talking to each other when they think no one in authority is listening.

Put together the desire and the maps, the broken pots and the mysterious words, a phrase of guttural music – but you have not found it. You are not there yet. Though the travellers come back and tell their tales and the scholars distil their theories and the explorers boast about the distant exotic places they have seen.

My country is somewhere else.

You pass through difficult places to get here because you've come the hard way, labouring over bleak tracks in bitter weather, looking so carefully for the hidden entrance between the bushes and the rocks. A narrow opening that you don't find because you are searching too hard and so you overlook it. Finding this out might take you many years but that's all right. Towards my continent you advance inch by inch. Others, wiser than you, who smoke hashish then close their eyes, dissolve in sweet smoke, lose themselves, and so arrive easily, coasting in on visions and dreams.

But for you, a trick is necessary. You need to trip, to wobble off-balance. You arrive unexpectedly. At this particular moment it's the last thing on your mind, coming here. You find it by accident. You fall into this place. Fall down, fall through, fall over, fall flat on your face. Once you've stretched out flat, feeling so low and so silly and so small – then wham! You're here.

It's all around you. Intense warmth as sunlight dances on water. The green fire of the trees encloses light, the leaves are illuminated from within.

Your feet follow the road you're on. Roads go ahead of you and show you the way. They mark out your desire. They are bearers of runs of colour and of white dust, flurries of chalk and of grey pebbles.

You're in a wide green valley terraced with orchards and fields, a silver river flowing in its deep crease. The road curves between plantations of cherries and tangerines and peaches. Cotton fields are ploughed, the land got ready for sowing.

You go through the valley, upwards, into the hills. Swiftly they surround you, small green mountains scattered with umbrella pines, higher mountains far on the horizon, blunt-topped, with rounded slopes calm as the flanks of sleeping animals, green dense as the fur on a cat's back.

A fertile landscape, well tended. A great garden, tilled and planted and pruned, irrigated by channels of water, walled by these mountains that melt into blue sky. One of those gardens you've seen in the background of old paintings, on the coloured pages of manuscripts. You crumble a fistful of earth in your palm, smell it. Slow warm shiver across your skin. I've

105

been here before I know this place I've come home. Images from dreams, the touch of sun and wind, somewhere once intimate and well-known, long since forgotten, now found again.

Judas trees shake purple flowers over you as you go by. Groves of olive trees behind dry-stone walls glitter grey-green and silver in the hot sunlight. The fruit trees in the orchards are in flower, rosy pink and pale pink and creamy white. Here and there among the green of the fields is a shout of scarlet, oblong beds of carnations massed together.

Groups of women sit under the trees. They wear brightly coloured baggy trousers, and loops of golden brass in their ears, and their long black hair topples down their backs. Some of them are sewing. Others strip the leaves from the long stems of artichokes. Donkeys and goats are tethered nearby, in the shade.

You meet few other travellers on the road in these burning hours. A flock of black sheep driven by a little girl with glossy dark plaits and silver ear-studs, and a gypsy, in a short red jacket, fastened with turquoise buttons, leading a bear with a long brown snout.

Sweat sluices you as you walk. You smell the peppery scent of freshly cut grass, the spicy clove perfume of the carnations, the green breath of the pines, the aniseed tang of wild fennel, the aromatic exhalations of rosemary and thyme.

You're hungry now, you look around for a picnic spot. On your left, just inside an overgrown meadow thick with marigolds, is a tumbledown bread oven, with a domed roof, like a tiny mosque. You settle yourself here to eat your slice of salty white cheese, bracelet of bread sprinkled with black poppy dots, handful of cracked green olives scented with lemon peel and crushed coriander seeds and garlic, couple of blue figs. Then you fall asleep, full of food, and the sun's heat, and the harshly sweet smell of marigolds and grass.

And when you wake, curled on the ground, it's there in front of you, the place you've been looking for; its great wall rearing up; behind it cluster the beehive tops of houses, the towers and spires of palaces and theatres and minarets. You've arrived. All you have to do is go in.

You cross courtyard after courtyard, one unfolding into another like the petals of a rose, you thread your way through a labyrinth of rooms and corridors. Like walking into a cut sapphire, the light refracts this way and that, you're happily lost.

You arrive in the central courtyard, open to the sky, arcaded, a fountain at its heart, its floor patterned by coloured pebbles into arabesques of pink, grey and white. The inner vaulting of the arcade is lined with mosaic of lapis lazuli and gold, and the outer face with blue and yellow tiles decorated with scrolls and fantastic birds. Above you, a row of pointed latticed windows, shut tight. Under your feet, as you peer into the cool gloom where the bright white sunlight cannot reach, is a pink and white and black marble pavement. In front of you, set into a fretted wooden frame in the green plastered wall, is a heavy door.

Did the sign, in flowing gilt letters cut into stone, say *Harem* or *Hammam* or something else? You blink, you refocus, you're past it, you're inside.

Smell of oranges and cardamom and mint. It's warm and dark. Tiny holes cut in the stone walls let lozenges of light spatter the pavement, so you're walking on and in a honeycomb of light. And this light swivels like a pencil, illuminating phrases and words carved into the stone. The light connects the words and phrases, a grammar of light, a prayer written by light on the walls and floor each hour of the day. To recite the Hours you walk up and down in here in the spangled darkness, slipping gold words like beads on to a shining thread. You're part of the gold net, you're dappled with points of light as you walk, the light loops you in, ties you up with knots of gold. Part of the prayer is to go barefoot, give yourself that pleasure walking in and out of patterns of warmth and coolness, darkness and light, you can pray with the soles of your feet.

In the dressing-room, its wood-panelled walls painted with red and yellow tulips, the dais in the centre heaped with striped cushions and mattresses, you strip off your clothes and hang them in the wardrobe lined with satiny cedarwood, sweet-smelling. Naked, you feel cheerful, anonymous. Nothing you have to carry with you. You pad through the curtained archway into the bath-house beyond.

107

Veils of mist close round you. Heat clothes you. Hot gossamer wraps your skin, presses on to your mouth. You can see nothing for the steam rising up in clouds, so you walk slowly, as though you're asleep, in a dream.

A doorway swims towards you and you part curtains of steam and go through, into another hot room. One vaulted stone room, dark with boiling steam, opens out of another, a labyrinth of heat. Already your breathing has slowed, as though hot wet cloths gag you, and your skin runs with water, as you start to dissolve into streams of sweat. Your toes nurse the hot pavement. Your eyes make out, through the billowing steam, stone beds around the walls, a clump of graceful columns in the centre, surrounded by stone chairs. You could be swimming, you're so loose in this tank of hot water that you could just float off, flick your tail, bump your nose on the carved ceiling.

The naked masseuse waiting for you in the furthest and hottest room is a big woman. Soft creased flesh of someone no longer young, silvery stretch-marks on her stomach. She steps delicately like a cat, pushing her wet hair off her face, beckons you in.

You lie down where she indicates, on the stone bench, letting the heat wash over you, into you. Steamy darkness, burning and fragrant. Nothing to do but slacken, flop, let go.

She heaves your arms and legs into position, arranges your head on one side, turned down, so that your cheek's on the warm wet towel. Her hands begin to squeeze and stroke the back of your neck, dawdle down your spine. She kneads and pinches and strokes. Kindness to the body. Her religion.

She slaps you, like wet clay, into shape. Her fingers seize and mould you, smoothe and pummel you. Joy flows up and down inside you like a river, explodes, flesh fireworks.

On your blissful skin the hands of the masseuse play a writing game. They spell out, in fingertalk, words and phrases, they trace love messages for your shut eyes to read:

ANON

mamabébé love you are here with you together us now over and over so
non-stop mamabébé so wanting you born this love us so close skinskin
talking heartbeat belonging with you allowed love home flesh my mamabébé our body singing to you so beautiful love listen mamabébé listen:

swimming in our waters we listen
to ourheartbeat

we is one whole undivided
you/me broken now mended
you/me restored mamabébé
our body of love pickedup putbacktogether
repaired
made whole again
by these us-hands
mamabébé
listen our bodysong:

stay mama stay bébé
stay mamabébé

born out of you
bébé born crying wanting you mamabébé
listen hush now bébé hush listen what mama say:

CHERUBINA

When you leave here, when you are born out of Paradise, you have to go out by one of two doors. One or the other. You have to choose. It's the way they do things out there. They like to see you coming out of one door or another. Then they know who you are, what kind of being, and what to think of you. Two arched doors in the wall, one next to the other. You can leave by only one of them. That's their rule out there. People find their own ways round it. They try to, anyway.

That city of theirs, that one out there, is famous for its beautiful buildings. White marble temples and houses and palaces set on a green hillside against a backdrop of blue sea and blue sky: newcomers marvel and exclaim, and the citizens gracefully accept their compliments.

If you descend the hillside, stepping carefully down the slippery white marble path, you come to one of the loveliest buildings in all the old city: the great Library, its façade decorated with tiers of white columns crowned with intricately carved capitals. It's a very large Library, for the city owns a noble collection of books, and is rich in scholars wishing to read them.

An equally large building is the municipal brothel, just across the road from the Library. Its façade is plain, all its decoration being on the inside, but still it is a substantial edifice, its design unpretentious and discreet according to the canons of good taste of the architects who built it.

The events I shall describe to you took place a little while ago.

In those days, the scholars went every day to the Library to study. Every morning, if they cared to check, the scholars' wives could watch their husbands tramp in through the great entrance to the Library, and every evening, if they wished to reassure themselves that their husbands' days had been well spent, they could watch them stumble out again, pallid from hours of close reading.

Unbeknownst to their wives, however, the enterprising scholars had dug a tunnel under the road, so that they could visit the brothel at any time of the day they chose, without being spotted, and find refreshment in the arms of the whores who worked there. If they came home at night pale after these bouts of pleasure their wives did not scold them but were innocently admiring of the hours their hard-working spouses put in studying in the Library.

So the scholars had a good life: books and sex combined, in exactly the ratio each one fancied, by day, and, at night, when they went home, there was supper ready, and a sympathetic wife.

In the dark hours before dawn the brothel closed its doors, to allow its inmates a chance to get their breath back after the rigours of the day and the evening just gone. The scholars departed. Everyone slept.

One night, however, one of the whores was too excited to sleep, for she had picked up a book accidentally left behind by one of the scholars and had begun to read it. All night long she sat reading and got to the last page just before breakfast-time.

She lent the book to her best friend in the brothel. It flew from hand to hand. The women discovered a taste for reading.

One book was not enough to keep them happy, though they all reread it several times. They needed more.

So in the middle of the night, in the dark hours before dawn, when everyone else in the city was asleep, the whores would get up, race down

112

the tunnel that connected the Library to the brothel, enter the Library, and spend the rest of the night there reading books.

So the existence of the tunnel benefited both parties. The whores could be in the Library by night and the scholars could be in the brothel by day. The scholars could sit in the Library, longing to finish a chapter so that they could nip under the road into the brothel and have a quick fuck, and the whores could lie in bed in the brothel, servicing the scholars, longing to finish the fuck so that they could dash under the road and have a quick read.

Cries of bliss echoed around the brothel by day and the Library by night.

Sometimes, now, whores and scholars met each other in the tunnel, racing in opposite directions. Sometimes the scholars raced the whores to see who could get to the Library first. Sometimes whores were discovered by scholars in the Library in the mornings, slumped half-asleep over their books. Sometimes the scholars stayed on all night in the brothel, hoping to tempt the whores away from their books.

For the whores no longer had their minds firmly fixed on their work. They had begun smuggling books back into the brothel with them, and could sometimes now be heard to say: just a sec, darling, I must just get to the end of this chapter.

— What are you reading now? the visiting scholar would ask.

— I'll read you a bit, shall I? the whore would reply, flicking backwards through the well-thumbed pages of her book: wait a minute, I've lost my place, oh yes here we are, now just listen to this:

Rosa

I crouched in my shivery place in the icy shed. The tarpaulin covering the sledge gleamed silvery-grey.

The little girls were quiet as though the snow had filled up their mouths. No call or cry from them. I thought I'd better look for them, see what trouble they might be in.

I stood up with a jerk, cramped and cold. I unbent my elbows and knees, one at a time. I knocked my hands together as though to punish them. I went out of the shed, into the garden.

I ploughed on into the meadow. I admit, I was afraid they had vanished or they were dead, that now I was alone and would die by myself in the snow. I almost started shouting for them, just to make a noise and feel a bit more alive, but then I saw them, at the far end of the meadow, walking round and round, lifting their boots high then stamping them down onto the white ground.

— We're going on a pilgrimage, they shouted, when they saw me: to see the holy places.

They broke their circle and ran to me. They were laughing as shrill as birds, excited.

Here in the meadow they had built *two* snowmen, side by side. The one from yesterday, finished now, with black coal eyes and mouth, a scarf round his neck, buttons like you make for gingerbread men in a neat row down his stomach. A pine cone for a nose, the snow shovel in his hands, my father's Sunday hat on his head, and a sprig of pine for a moustache.

Next to him stood the snow-woman, his bride. They had given her hair of pine twigs, and a wreath of mistletoe on top. Her hands clasped a nosegay of ivy and holly. She was solid, well built in snow, with her coal mouth crooked into a smile.

Just enough room was left between the two statues for the little girls to run in and out, shouting with laughter, and to dance their pilgrimage dance around, in a figure of eight. Let them play, I thought. Stop them thinking about how we are starving.

The angel was hungry too. I felt her fist between my shoulder blades. A blow that drove me back to the shed, to its chill darkness.

A cold place with no light. It was empty. There could be no spark of life in here. Only death would find it suitable. It was death's waiting-room. Death waited for me, with sharp teeth, ready to pounce and tear into my flesh.

The shed wasn't empty. As my eyes grew used to the grey dimness I saw the sledge still standing there. With the long wrapped bundle frozen on to it. A bier, bearing a dead body parcelled up in a grey tarpaulin shroud.

I knelt down by the sledge and burst into tears. My mother was dead and I had done it. It was my fault. She used to shout at me: oh do stop saying sorry. Now she would never shout at me again. It was too late to ask her for forgiveness. She hid on the sledge, cold meat, bloodless.

The tears fell from my eyes in salt streams. They stung my face, they were so hot. They scorched my cheeks, then landed on the tarpaulin fastened over the sledge. Puddles of tears on its iced blankness. Patches here and there that began to melt, the water I wept was so heated, my sorrow so stoked up.

The sheen of ice masking the great tarpaulin dissolved. A lake of tears dripped to the floor. I stretched out a hand and pulled the cold grey covering away from the sledge. It fell, crackling, to the floor.

Underneath was a long block of ice.

A windowpane of ice separated us. Like a glass, transparent. My mother was embedded in ice. She stared back at me, wide-eyed, her face frozen into a cry of surprise she couldn't make. Ice between her lips, a sliver of ice-bread. A Communion Host fragile as a snowflake.

She was wearing only a white petticoat. Her limbs suspended in pearly ice. Like when you go to the fishmonger and see freshly caught fish, wet, lit with silver and blue, on the marble slab packed about with crushed whiteness, cold gleams. She was waiting. What else could she do? Almost a mermaid, so remote and so beautiful. The winter had taken her, she rested in its cold grip, its deathly arms.

She was preserved in freshness. I couldn't touch her. I couldn't reach through the ice. She floated in it mildly, she was adrift, far off, in some private place. Surprised, and dreaming, with wide-open eyes. She couldn't see me. Ice gleamed on her like moonlight.

The ice wanted to prevent me. It talked: no no no no.

I got as close to her as I could. I put my lips to the ice that held and surrounded her like love. I kissed her. My lips burned and blistered on the casing of ice. I kissed her again and again, I sucked and bit her glass flesh, I threw my salt tears on to her, to make her cool surface start to melt, I drove my kisses at her, I hammered an iron spike of crying into that ice block and shivered it to splinters, I made her dissolve, I got to her, I held her in my arms and nibbled and licked her, my waterfall, in her cold current I would not freeze, I would not drown, I would warm her and warm her up and she would be safe and dry and hold me and I would not be hungry any more.

The mask of ice that moulded her face blurred at the edges. It melted, and slid off. Her buckler and breastplate of ice turned to slush, to water. Her gauntlets of ice fell from her hands.

All night long, I thought, the sledge had travelled of its own volition, no driver, no horse. Through the darkness it sped on its runners of bright steel, it glided over the hissing ice, it drove straight at our house and returned our mother to us. She was tied to us by invisible ropes. She had not been able to get free.

Her eyelids creaked up and down. She saw me. She switched her gaze to something that trembled behind me. I turned round. My father stood in the doorway, with the little girls.

When she sighed, crisps of ice that had covered her eyelids curved down her face, cracked tears. My mother hardly ever cried. Now I saw her sorrow as she wept. Tears spilled down her face and she shivered and cried some more. I knew she hated us seeing her cry.

I wondered where she had been and what she had seen. I wanted her to tell us all that. First the ice kept us apart but now it connected us. I wanted to hear her melting words, her words of heated ice.

In through the door came pale sunshine, a breath of warmth, the scent of green things sprouting. The spring crept up on us. Deep in the trees I heard the wood pigeons coo and burr, the lively chatter of tits. The sun increased in strength. Like two warm hands that caressed your face. I could smell fresh grass, I could smell the earth full of greenery.

My mother sat up. She who had been dead returned to life and sat up. That is the miracle I have seen. My mother restored to live with us alive and beautiful and young like the green world in spring when the snow melts and the coldness goes away.

My mother opened her mouth and began to speak. My mother told us the story of why she came back, a tale of danger and rescue:

FEDERIGO

This afternoon my father fetched me from my mother's room, where I was playing cards with her and two other ladies, and gave me this book. He said I am to write in it, first of all to please myself and so gain practice in the art of writing, and later on, at a time he will decide upon, at his bidding. He will require me to take notes of what I see and hear, and to write at his dictation an account of everything that passes.

Though I know what he means, I pretended that I did not, to spare him more suffering. For his face was all red as he spoke to me, his voice constricted. I know how dearly he loves the Abbess, my sister, and that he wishes to save her if he can. Though I also know he fears that now there is nothing any of us can do. For my part I shall show my affection for my father by writing as close an account as I can of the Inquiry, when it begins. I shall become his clerk, and provide him with a record translated from Latin into the plainest and clearest phrasing possible. Later on he will be able to study it at his leisure, and examine to his own satisfaction the evidence presented each day. I think he hopes to enlist the Bishop's help, but my mother says he

118

should be doubtful of this. She did not say more in front of me. She took my father's arm and walked with him away into the garden.

I shall obey my father and practise remembering things that are done and said and then can be written down privily in this book. I shall begin by writing down at night what I have done that day. It feels strange, and not a little foolish, to make the subject of my writing the trifling details of my daily life. When, during the past months, I have written stories to amuse my mother and sisters, they are always chivalric romances such as I first met with in the house of the Contessa, concerned with the feats of heroes, of men of honour. However, to please my father, I shall try to master this new kind of writing.

This morning I woke early. I accompanied my mother and sisters to Mass, then attended them while they walked to meet some other ladies and talk to them. I left them and went into the piazza and walked about with my father and the companions he was conversing with.

My father dined with these gentlemen, having further business with them. I went home and dined with my mother. Esterina Gonzo had made my mother one of her favourite dishes, to try and give her pleasure. Sausages made from the pig killed at Christmas, flavoured with sage and juniper, served on a bed of lentils with lemon and olive oil. It is an excellent dish, but my mother's appetite was not as hearty as usual.

I longed to go out, but I stayed with my mother because I could see she was oppressed by sadness though she strove to hide it. To distract her, I made her play cards with me. Then Esterina came up and said that two of my mother's friends were below. They came in and joined us at cards.

My father fetched me out and took me into his room where he keeps all his books and writes his letters. He gave me this book which he got for me this morning from the stationer. He said he would read what I wrote in it. Then he made me kneel before him and swear to serve him faithfully in this matter of writing. Then he prayed to Almighty God that I, his only son, should always live an honourable life and not bring disgrace upon the family as my poor sister had done. Then he embraced me and went away to walk with my mother who had come to find him, her ladies being gone.

2 September

I intended to write in this book every day, but I have not. It is too difficult, because so repetitive and so trifling, to put down the events of the household. Also I do not wish to sadden my father, when he comes to read this, with too accurate a picture of the grief and shame afflicting us all. My little sisters are too young to understand.

I spent most of the last week studying, and got on very well. Attendance at the Inquiry will test my capacity in Latin and then in fluent writing. I would rather be out with my friends and our horses and dogs, but I am sure it is God's will that I do this instead.

Father Giovanni walked back with us after Mass this morning, and stayed to dinner. We had tomorrow's dinner instead of today's, which was polenta with mushroom sauce. Instead we ate the quails I shot, with a very good sauce with wine in it, and the birds wrapped in sprigs of rosemary before roasting. Esterina Gonzo flattened them with a wooden mallet before cooking them. She made me come into the kitchen and help her, my sisters being too young to be of good use to her and my mother with her best clothes on being anyway occupied in other arrangements for dinner.

Esterina told me, while we were preparing the birds together, that yesterday she gave one of the prison guards money and asked him for news of my sister the Abbess, how she was faring in her imprisonment. The guard told her my sister never speaks, but she is well enough, though she is allowed no exercise and sleeps on a pallet on the floor, with none of the luxury she was formerly used to. They have taken away her religious habit and put a penitent's dress on her. But they have allowed her a companion, one of her nuns, to share her cell, Sister Giuditta, who was accused together with my sister Bona.

Esterina Gonzo said that the guard told her that Sister Giuditta had orders to spy on my sister during these days, to see how she conducted herself. Esterina said I should tell all this to my parents, to comfort them. But she dared not tell them herself in case they punished her for going to the prison and talking to the guard. She said she got the money to pay him from a friend.

I accused her of committing immodest and lewd acts with the guard to persuade him to give her the information and she began crying and calling on Our Lady to swear to her good name and conduct. My mother came in, asking what all the noise was about, so we stopped talking. I would not tell her what Esterina said. I let her think Esterina had spoken insolently to me, so my mother boxed her on the ears and went away again. I shall not tell my father either, because it would only distress him. When he reads this account in some days' time, it will be soon enough. So I gave Esterina some money for her trouble. I gave her a kiss also, because I cannot forget she was my nurse once, even if she is old now and sometimes behaves foolishly. She said she would tell my mother herself of her visit to the prison.

4 September

My mother stayed in bed, indisposed. We gave her tisane. I took the little girls in to her, when she asked for them, for her amusement.

I remembered of course who Sister Giuditta is, for I have seen her. She was the nun at the convent who acted as assistant to the old nun at the postern gate and helped take in packages and letters. On Wednesdays she sold cakes the nuns had made, passing them through the little door in the gate. She collected the money payment first, then put the cake on the flat wheel fixed in the little door, with a black curtain hiding half of it so that you could not see her face, and spun the wheel and so sent the cake out to you. That was Giuditta. I know, because she had a very sweet voice my mother remembered, and now remarked upon. My mother asked her name and she told us. My mother exclaimed, and asked for her prayers. That was many months ago, when my sister the Abbess still allowed guests to talk through the grille to the nuns in the parlour, before she closed the convent doors and let nobody from the outside come in. We could not go in that day, because it was not yet the end of Holy Week, but we could send my

121

sister in a present of lemons and pickles, and we could buy the cake. It was for Easter Sunday. It was a special almond cake, which the nuns know how to make very well. My mother wrapped it in a cloth and put it in a basket and we took it home. It was made not only with almonds but had orange peel and nutmeg and sultanas in it and chips of white sugar. When we cut the cake on Easter Sunday and ate it I picked out two of the sultanas and put them on the side of my plate. They were as round and black as Sister Giuditta's eyes when she lifted the corner of the black curtain and peeped at me. At the time when I first knew her I was a boy merely, whereas now I am a man.

I remembered this because I had to help Esterina Gonzo with her baskets and parcels. I had to carry some of them home for her. She had two bales of cloth, black and white, as well as a bag of flour, and they were too heavy for her. She laughed at me because I had accused her of tempting the guard, whereas she is as old as my mother and grew up with her on the farm at Povizzo. When we came across the piazza we saw the arrival of the Inquisitors, in a stately procession, with Father Giovanni amongst them carrying a tall cross. We stopped and said a prayer and so came home. On the way I remembered how I had seen Sister Giuditta two years ago. The sunlight glittering on the cross, and the black cloth under Esterina's arm, made me think of it. I do not know why I have written that down since it is a foolish matter. Writing this record is more difficult that I thought it would be. Sometimes the sentences come out very strangely and look disordered. It will be easier when I have mastered how to put things down in the right order. My father repeated to me at dinner that he wished me to continue with this practice, so I am obeying him. For dinner we had the fish I brought home, with caper sauce, very good, baked in a closed dish. My mother would not eat, because she is indisposed.

5 September

It being Sunday we went out to Mass. On the way we met two of my father's friends, and stopped to talk with them. The chief of the Inquisitors, the Monsignor, said Mass. He wore a green cope embroidered with gold, very beautiful and fine. He was assisted by two others, Father Giovanni and Father Sebastiano Bagolan, and three more Dominicans at the side. I have not seen Father Sebastiano for many months. On the way out of church, when we had stopped to greet my father's friend Terenzio Covolo, I saw that Father Sebastiano saw us but he chose not to know us. He turned his head away.

In his sermon the Monsignor spoke of the need for renewal and for faith in our Holy Mother Church, who, being free of errors, can safely lead us out of the Devil's snares. The Mass was in thanksgiving for the miraculous and safe return of the holy relics of Santa Salome after their exile for some years in the chapel of my sister's convent. Now they are to go to the cathedral in Grezzano. The Monsignor showed us the reliquary like a burning tree, all of gold, like a monstrance, indeed, for displaying the sacred Host. Each golden leaf on this golden tree, which had the form of the burning bush in which God hid while He spoke to our holy father Moses, contained a little window in it, with the particular relic being visible behind, wrapped in cloth like bandages. The Monsignor held the reliquary while each of us came forward and kissed it in turn, to show our duty to God and to His emissaries the Holy Inquisition.

When my turn came to kneel and kiss the holy box I was so strongly moved by the sacred nature of the occasion that I wanted to weep, but dared not for fear that the Monsignor would remember me afterwards too well and perhaps call me for questioning. I think it was God moving in my heart, and moving me to tears of compassion for my poor sister. Whatever she has done, I heartily pray to God to forgive her and to rescue her from future sin. I fear for her grievously if she is found guilty of whatever they accuse her of. I do not know precisely what that is, and shall not until after the Inquiry begins. Then we came out of church and Father Sebastiano would not look at us.

We dined on fried liver done with onions and rice and herbs, very good. Today my mother put on her best clothes and came to eat with us, to show her duty to my father. She spoke to him tenderly. The little girls were much affected by the melancholy of the rest of us and made more noise than usual. So my mother gave them a plate of walnuts and sent them outside to eat them in the garden. Later we heard them playing very merrily with the dogs. Tomorrow I shall cease this practice record of our domestic life, for the Inquiry begins. My father says the Contessa will be coming to attend it, for as the patroness of the convent she is very concerned about its affairs. Indeed, as I know very well, it was she who began the proceedings that led to my sister's discovery.

6 September

This morning when I went in to my mother she was composed. She said she had not slept all night. She was busy with her sewing. So I left her, and the little girls busy with Esterina playing with the pots and pans in the kitchen, and went with my father to join the great throng of people in the piazza. Some of them had been there for a long time, hoping for a good place. All fell back to let the procession of the Inquisitors pass inside, and the Contessa with her men about her and two ladies.

We followed in their wake. We found seats on the last bench at one side. The common people stood like cowed cattle in the middle, turning their heads this way and that and buzzing like cattle flies until the clerk told them to be quiet. I kept my commotion inside my own heart but I believe it was the same as theirs, at such a spectacle of solemnity and authority as those most high Inquisitors seated far above us on the dais in their sober robes.

I kept this book in my pocket, and a bit of pencil ready in my hand concealed until I should want to use it. I tried to remember everything that was said, and not to need recourse to writing, for fear I should be seen and ordered to give up my book for scrutiny. I believe I succeeded, for I think I shall be able to put down here now those things said which will be of use to my father going over what passed.

They spoke to Father Giovanni first, their questions to him being recorded by the three clerks, the Dominicans, and also everything that he said in reply. So I shall write down only the things that he spoke, in an

124

accurate form I hope, but a shortened one, to save my hand from getting cramped. Father Sebastiano Bagolan, I must not forget to say, sat at the table as one of the three clerks, just below the dais where the Monsignor sat with the other two Inquisitors. He was very pale. He did not look at me.

I shall omit the formalities with which the Inquiry began, because my father was there and could hear them very well for himself. Also it would take too long to put them all down here. I will go on to what came next.

Father Giovanni was required to answer the questions put to him. I shall not write the questions, but only the answers.

Father Giovanni said that he served the parish of Santa Salome as parish priest and had done for thirty years. He was fifty years of age. He had served the convent of Santa Salome as chaplain to the nuns for seven years, since the foundation of the house by the Contessa with the approval of our Holy Mother Church. He had been prevented by the Abbess, Sister Bona Casolin, from fulfilling his duties to herself and her nuns for the last year, in flagrant breach of the holy Rule given to the nuns by His Eminence the Bishop of Grezzano. The Rule specified that the Abbess should submit her judgement and will at all times to that of the Chaplain, who represented the authority of our Holy Mother Church and in particular that of His Eminence. Father Giovanni considered that the Abbess, Sister Bona Casolin, had flouted not only the holy Rule prescribed for her, but also canon law.

Sister Bona Casolin had stopped letting Father Giovanni hear her confession, and she had stopped the other nuns from confessing also. She had begun to call herself their spiritual director and had assumed responsibility for the care and guidance of their souls.

Sister Bona had stopped taking Holy Communion and had stopped the other nuns from taking it also. Then she had stopped hearing Mass altogether, and had commanded the other nuns to do likewise.

She had removed the precious reliquary containing the relics of Santa Salome from the convent chapel to the oratory adjoining her cell, in order, she said, that she could benefit from their healing presence should she be awake in the night and wish to say her prayers. When Father Giovanni said he would keep the reliquary for her in a locked cupboard in the sacristy, even so she had refused to give it back. Shortly afterwards she had bolted the side door into the convent, through which Father Giovanni normally entered when he came in to say Mass and advise the Abbess and hear the nuns' confessions. She would not allow him to come in again.

A woman should not do these things. It was a grave sin for her to usurp the authority vested in her superiors.

Father Giovanni said that Sister Bona Casolin also committed perverse and lewd acts with the other nuns, in which she usurped the natural function of a man. He saw her commit this sin when he watched through the sacristy keyhole at a time when the nuns had gone into the chapel to sing the Office of Matins. He saw them half-naked and the Abbess too, behaving immodestly with them. He could not see all that they did because they moved out of his sight into the choir-stalls. Soon after this the Abbess bolted the side door and would not let him come back in again.

That was the first day of the Inquiry. My father and I walked home by a back way, not wanting to meet our friends. I shall not report all that we said to one another, because it is only this matter of the Inquiry that concerns my writing now. Esterina told me she took food to the prison for my sister. Two of the Dominicans were there. They had vowed to visit her every afternoon to pray for her soul, and that she would repent.

7 September

The second day of the Inquiry. Again, we took our seats at the back of the benches on the right, where we could see and hear very well what went on but remain inconspicuous, as far as possible.

Sister Giuditta was called, she being the confidante of the Abbess during their time together in the convent, and now also her close companion in prison. She was brought up to the dais by two guards. She was in penitent's dress, her habit having been taken away from her. She was bare-headed, with her hair cut very short.

126

Sister Giuditta said that her parents put her into the convent when it was founded, since they had several other daughters and so not enough money to give her a dowry to get her married. She knew the Abbess before, when they were playmates together when they were girls. This was in the days before the convent was founded, when they were seven or eight years old.

I remember this so clearly that I am impelled to write it down, even though I know I should not. I remember Giuditta coming to our house to see my sister. They called to me and I went to join their games, because they had invited me to play with them. At that time I was five or thereabouts. I found them in the bakehouse behind the kitchen where there was the great oven in which my mother cooked her bread and cakes. It was dark when I went in and I could not see. They had closed the doors. They caught me in their hands and made me play with them. They were playing weddings. I had to be the husband. First with my sister and then with Giuditta. Each time while the other one watched. We played that game four times. My sister said I wedded Giuditta too eagerly, so she stopped us. We could smell the cake in the oven was almost done, so we ran away before my mother could catch us. It was a good place to play because it was very warm. Later on my sister got clouted by Esterina Gonzo because she forgot to warn her the cakes were done and they burnt and that made my mother very angry. I promised my sister to tell no one what we did. But the next time that Giuditta came to our house she and my sister would not let me join their games but went off in secret. And after that Giuditta came always only to see my sister and would not play with me again as she had.

What I have just written is a great piece of foolishness. It is a story I have told no one. Now I have told it to this book I shall tear out the page before my father comes to read it.

Sister Giuditta said in the Inquisition that she was nineteen years old and had been in the convent for seven years. For some time she had held the keys to the postern gate. On Sundays and feast days she opened the door to the families and friends of the nuns, who were permitted to visit the nuns in the parlour, and talk to them there through the grille. At other times she took in messages and parcels and letters, by means of the wheel fixed in the gate, and sent out the same. Sister Giuditta said that Sister Bona Casolin kept the rule of enclosure very strictly. She kept the world out. The only males allowed in were the nuns' close relatives, and they could go no further than the parlour. Even the Chaplain, Father Giovanni, was permitted only into the sacristy, by means of the side door, and thence into the chapel, but no further. One year ago or thereabouts, Sister Bona stopped all these visits. She told Sister Giuditta that the Bishop was sending spies to spy upon her and find fault with her house and how she ruled it, and she wished to defend herself against this.

Sister Giuditta said that the Abbess was a loving and indulgent Mother to her daughters in Christ. She allowed the novices to play games, for example, for they were very young, and she said that merry hearts loved God well. She allowed them, while they polished the floors with cloths tied to their bare feet, to play at a mock tournament, a joust of Mothers against Daughters tilting with mops. Or she let them play at a foolish sort of cookery, with each novice choosing the name of a food, calling herself Onion or Fennel or Parsley, and so on, and then choosing to dance in groups, so that different foods came newly together, when Almond might dance with Aubergine and Orange, and so these dances were called Recipes, and named new dishes to please the Abbess's fancy. This childish and absurd practice was to encourage the cook to be inventive and constantly to search for fresh lively menus with which to tempt the nuns' appetites.

Sister Giuditta said that this was in order to combat the deadly sin of *accidie*. She said the Abbess said that if the nuns were bored they might succumb to spiritual despair.

Sister Giuditta said that if any one of them had cause for rejoicing, such as the feast day of her patron saint, or her birthday, or some anniversary to do with her entry into religious life, she was given permission to enjoy a Little Feast, and to invite all the Sisters to share it with her. A Little Feast meant especially good food to eat, and sitting talking in the garden, and

128

then dancing and singing in the evening, and playing the drum and the tambourine.

A Great Feast was held for Midsummer's Day, and the winter solstice, and the spring equinox, and the Abbess's birthday, and other occasions Sister Giuditta forgot.

Sister Giuditta said that the Abbess had dispensed the nuns from too much fasting, because she believed it damaged their health, and from eating only one meal, of fish, on Fridays. Those who wanted meat could have it, just as those who wanted wine at supper-time could have more than just half a glass.

The Abbess said that it was too cold in the chapel to say the Night Office there. She invited those who wanted to join her in her cell at that time, where she kept a fire burning all night, and so they could be warm. She kept the reliquary containing the relics of Santa Salome in her oratory, next to her cell, and she said they could pray very well in there.

Sister Giuditta wept and said Sister Bona Casolin did not worship the Devil and did not practise witchcraft. She did not ape the priest's role and she did not say a Black Mass.

Sister Giuditta was often the Abbess's companion at night, out of kindness, and the obedience she owed her Superior under Holy Rule. She often slept in her bed with her, to keep her warm at night, because the convent was very cold in winter, even with the fire that the Abbess caused to be kept burning in the grate. Often the other nuns did not join them to sing the Night Office in the little oratory, preferring to stay asleep in their beds, and the Abbess allowed them to do that. She only insisted they come to her cell and pray at night with her on the occasions of Great Feasts. She said that those who needed to sleep should do so.

She was not a lax Superior. When she had to punish someone, she could be severe. She loved her daughters in Christ, and desired to perfect them, and so she punished them when necessary. She did not allow them to wear hair shirts or spikes in private, and she would not suffer them, either, to use the discipline over their naked shoulders, in private, on Friday nights, as the Rule said they should. She said this might be abused by the more zealous

129

among the Sisters. Instead she had the wrongdoer brought to her cell, or any Sister desiring punishment for some misdeed. This happened very rarely, only three or four times in seven years as Sister Giuditta could recall.

What happened on those occasions was that the Abbess had the walls of her cell hung with cloths of scarlet. These cloths were very fine and good, and were used for no other purpose. Afterwards they were taken down and folded away in the press.

They were supposed to signify the suffering and Passion of Our Lord when he was tried then scourged by Pilate.

It was Sister Giuditta who pinned up the cloths beforehand, then took them down after. The bell rang, and all the nuns assembled. Though it was night, they wore their habits, and kept their faces hidden with their veils pulled forward.

At other times, as for example on the occasions of Little and Great Feasts, the Abbess permitted her nuns to leave off their veils and coifs and let their hair flow over their shoulders. She said she liked to see their hair, which was the crowning glory of virgins giving themselves to Christ their Spouse. Also when they were singing the Office in choir she liked them to leave off their veils and coifs and instead to wear the crowns of gold wire she had made for them. She said these crowns were more fitting for the brides of Christ. It was only on these few occasions of punishment, very strange and very terrible, that she insisted the nuns be fully clothed as the Rule specified, though it was the middle of the night.

It was called the Sacrament of Penitence. Sister Giuditta had received it once. The Abbess punished her for leaving the oratory door unlocked and letting Sister Zita have access to the reliquary in the oratory, which she stole.

All the Sisters stood around the walls of the cell of their Mother, which was draped in red. Sister Bona Casolin received the penitent gently, making her kneel in front of her, then cutting a slit in her habit at the front and back and pulling it until she was naked above the waist with her clothes hanging down. Her veil and coif were taken off and her hair bound up on her head, very high. She was caused to lie forwards, over the Abbess's knees, resting against them, her own knees on the floor, her breasts against the knees of the Abbess and her head in her lap, in the posture of a child who is tired and seeks rest, or to be picked up.

With one arm the Abbess held the penitent in a gesture of tenderness and with the other she wielded a whip and whipped her.

Not over-hard. Just enough to hurt her enough. Not very many times. Just enough to frighten her and the others. And all the time the Abbess cradled her while she beat her. It was called penitence, and it was called the Passion, because it felt thick and red, like blood. It was terrible and it was delightful, though it did hurt.

She was held tightly, as though in bonds, yet they were bonds of tenderness.

All the others watched the blows fall on the naked back of the penitent held lightly against her Mother's knees.

There could be a very sweet feeling in it.

Afterwards they would all go back to bed and sleep. And as like as not next day there might be a Little Feast for some reason. Because to come through the Sacrament of penitence was to make an advance in the religious life. It was to go deeper in. So there was a celebration.

Sister Giuditta could not remember anything else.

I could not let my father see how much this recital excited me. So at the close of the day's Inquiry I pretended to be feeling sick and ran home alone. I stood in the bakehouse and thought of Giuditta violently. Then when it was over I heard my mother calling me and came in. Later I will tear this out and recopy the part of it which is seemly. My father and I have not spoken of what Giuditta said. Later I will burn some of this. This evening my mother was calm, and did not cry at all. She said she had spent the day at prayer, and sewing, and that Esterina Gonzo had helped her with all the things she had to do about the house. She said none of her friends had come to see her as they usually did. She had desired them to stay away while the Inquiry was in progress, because she slept badly at night and had bad dreams, and by day was unfit for her friends' company. She preferred to stay quietly by herself with the little girls and with Esterina. So we all said a prayer together and went to bed.

131

8 September

The Monsignor asked Father Sebastiano Bagolan to stand up.

Again I shall omit the questions put to him by the Holy Fathers of the Inquisition, and record only his replies.

He said that he had been in the service of the Contessa for three years, since his ordination as a priest, as her secretary. Then, during this last year, by the grace and inspiration of God, he had discovered his vocation to the Dominican Order, in which Order he now served. He now lived in the Dominican monastery near Padua with his brothers, and he served as one of the clerks to the Most Holy Inquisition at Padua. He had arrived in Santa Salome with the other Fathers a week ago.

Father Sebastiano said that since his arrival he had diligently gone about the village here questioning the inhabitants in order to discover some witnesses to the terrible events that precipitated the arrival of himself and the other Fathers of the Inquisition in this place.

He said he was referring to the reports sent to the Bishop and to the Contessa. They were sent by Father Giovanni, who had not seen these things himself but thought he ought to report that others said that their neighbours said these things were happening.

Father Sebastiano said: naked men with their genitals torn off, babies mutilated and bleeding, naked women with their breasts torn off, howling and crying at night. Body parts seized by red-hot pincers, dismembered bodies hacked up then flung violently about.

He believed that the people of these parts were more than ordinarily credulous, ignorant, and superstitious, it being such a poor and mountainous region, so remote that the winds of reform and renewal blowing through the Church had not yet reached it. The religious beliefs and practises of these people showed how much they stood in need of the cleansing and purging relief offered by the Inquisition. They believed, for example, that the recent terrible epidemic, which took the lives of so many, was a punishment for sin sent by God, and that the siege of Mantua, in which so many died, was also a scourging from God.

132

Father Sebastiano said that these lowly and foolish people could not properly understand the sermons preached by their priest, Father Giovanni Girotto, every Sunday in church, upon subjects such as the Massacre of the Innocents, and their subsequent life in Limbo, and the tortures of the damned awaiting those reserved a place in Hell after death. They had begun to believe that the end of the world was nigh. They had begun to believe that they were living in Hell and that therefore the tortures practised by the fiends upon the bodies of sinners were being inflicted now upon the bodies of the living. They were so gripped by their fear of damnation, and of the punishments awaiting them in Hell, that they thought they saw wicked souls being carried off all around them, to be plunged into the fire for all eternity. They believed the Devil walked amongst them, to snatch souls.

Father Sebastiano said he was certain that the sins of the Abbess and her companions in the convent were not of that sort he had just described, which had been carried to the convent's door by gossip and rumour. The sins of the Abbess were of a different kind.

Offences against Holy Rule and against canon law. Also heretical beliefs and practices.

He knew this from the report given by Sister Zita Consolaro of what she witnessed in the convent.

Sister Zita could not be called to speak to the Inquiry.

She had died, following a severe fever, shortly after her escape from the convent of Santa Salome and her arrival at the house of Dominican nuns near Padua. She had been placed in the infirmary there by the good sisters. Before her death she had made her confession and received the Last Sacrament, and she had dictated a report of what happened while she was in the convent to Father Sebastiano himself. He came to the infirmary every day to give what comfort he could to the sick and dying. He had asked to be allowed to do this, ever since his acceptance by the Dominicans into their house near that of the nuns, to show his gratitude to God for his vocation.

Sister Zita Consolaro was a young widow, friendless and penniless. Because of her devotion to Santa Salome, the patroness of wandering women, she had asked to enter the convent at Santa Salome. She had asked for asylum and had been taken in as an object of charity. Though it was too soon for her to make her vows she was allowed to wear the habit, and she was called Sister Zita by all the nuns, as though she were really one of them. This was customary behaviour towards one not yet professed.

In her report she testified to those things already said by Sister Giuditta Baston. She also observed all those things with her own eyes. She was much troubled by them. She prayed very much about them, to know what she should do. She was very dismayed to discover that the holy relics of Santa Salome had been removed from the chapel into the oratory of the Abbess. She did not dare remonstrate with the Abbess, for fear of her violent temper which was easily provoked. The other nuns were all frightened of the Abbess and would do nothing. She discovered that the convent gates were barred against everyone, including the chaplain Father Giovanni Girotto, and so she could tell no one what she saw.

Sister Bona Casolin, the Abbess, said her own Mass. She said it at night, in the oratory adjoining her cell. Sister Giuditta Baston was often there and assisted her. Sister Zita saw them.

Sister Bona Casolin said this Mass at her whim, sometimes in the evening of the holiday she caused to happen to mark the beginning of female impurity. This began for all the nuns together on the same day every month. There was a Little Feast held, with those who wanted to resting in bed and others allowed to do as they pleased, reading books or playing shuttlecock in the orchard or washing each other's hair in the bath-house. Then on that first night the Abbess would sometimes say her Mass, if she felt like it. This blasphemous act was called a Great Feast.

The Abbess was very fond of acting and dressing up. She encouraged the other nuns to follow her in this. She wrote plays which they performed.

She said her Mass over the reliquary containing the precious relics of Santa Salome. In the beginning she used to say the Mass in the convent chapel, but after Father Giovanni Girotto watched her through the sacristy keyhole she locked the convent gates against him and began to say the Mass upstairs. Sister Zita did not witness the Abbess's Mass in the chapel. Sister

Giuditta told her about it. It happened before Sister Zita came to the convent. She was a witness of three of the Great Feasts upstairs.

She could see what happened, because there was firelight in the cell, and there were candles, and oil-lamps taken from the shelf outside the refectory. These lit the oratory.

Those who were there wore the crowns of gold wire the Abbess had made for them. They wore their hair flowing and loose, after drying it in the sun, after their bath. They sang the canticle in praise of Santa Salome which the Abbess had written. Sister Zita Consolaro joined in because she was afraid not to.

The Abbess committed sacrilegious and blasphemous acts. She opened the reliquary and held the broken bits of relics in her hands and prayed over them. She said that these were the body of our Mother. She said that we broke her with our sins of anger. Then seeing her destroyed we felt very wicked.

The Abbess held out her hands with the bits of relics in them. She said: I am the body of love. I am the garden, walled and enclosed, in which you flourish, and I am the earth that holds you when you die. I am the body in which you are reborn, the garden where you grow again.

The Abbess bared her breast. She said: this is my body, which was broken and given for you, and this is my blood, which was shed for you. My body and blood gave you life and shall give you life and lead you to life and lead you back into life. I will pour out my riches upon you and give you my treasures and anoint you with my precious oils. Then you will be healed and mended and raised up, and I too shall be made whole and restored.

Then each of the nuns came forward and kissed the Abbess's breast, and let her mouth rest there, as though she was an infant being nursed by her mother. The Abbess in her depravity and wickedness called this a sacrament and the true sacrament of Holy Communion.

Sister Zita forced herself to participate in this disgusting ritual three times, so that none should suspect her. Each time afterwards she fell down in a faint. Sister Giuditta said to her that this was caused by the power of bliss but this was not true.

135

Sister Zita left the convent of Santa Salome because of what she saw and heard there. She took the reliquary with the bones of Santa Salome in it, from the oratory next to the Abbess's cell, to save them from being mocked. She went away early in the morning, while all the others were asleep. She unbolted the gate and slipped out. No one saw her or tried to stop her. She hastened towards Padua, because she knew there were the two houses of Dominicans there where she could ask for sanctuary. The sisters took her in. Later on they buried her and had Masses said for her soul. Father Sebastiano said: Sister Zita had vanished, to a better home than this one, in heaven. He said that he prayed often for her soul.

Tomorrow being a feast day and a holiday, the Inquisition is halted. On the following day they will call my sister Bona before them and then they will decide what to do with her and Sister Giuditta, whether they should be burned. The other nuns are all dispersed, to convents nearby. They are not seen as culpable in the same way. They were led astray by Bona, to whom in any case they were vowed in obedience, and by Giuditta.

We hurried home by the roundabout way, having come out of the Inquiry by the back door. My father's friends did not have time to reach him to talk with him. He was too ashamed that they should see him, after what we heard today. He did not tell me this but I knew what he felt. He bit his lip and did not speak to me. My mother came out to meet us and embraced us both and clasped us by the hand. She told us to keep faith with God and with each other. She took my father a little way apart, saying: trust me.

Later on I went and walked about in the garden, in some distress of mind. I did not know whether to tell my father what I knew about Father Sebastiano, for fear I should also tell him those things I should not, about what happened on the road when we travelled with the pilgrims down from Fiacenza back here to Santa Salome. All he knows is what I told him, that I came home in the company of the pilgrims for safety on the journey, being, the Contessa thought, too young to travel alone. Before we set off, the Contessa made me swear silence about it all. She promised in return to save my sister and not to let her fall into the Inquisitors' hands. She said

136

Father Sebastiano would save her. I believed her, and so I swore. No one here knows of the part played by Father Sebastiano in it all. That is why he would not know me in church last Sunday. If I tell what I know, no one will believe me. It will perhaps cause my sister even greater harm. Yet my silence grieves me. It presses on me. My only relief is writing down some of those things here.

I was walking up and down throwing bread into the fish pond to amuse my little sisters. They love the bright red-gold colours of the carp. Esterina came out and stood with us. She said my father had sent a message to Father Giovanni, and to Father Sebastiano and the other Dominican clerks, to ask them to dine with us tomorrow noon. He begged it as a great favour to himself, the poor father of a sinner, that they would show compassion and mercy on him by coming to eat. Esterina was sure they would come, since Father Giovanni's house, where they are lodged, is so cramped and draughty, and he cannot afford to give them very good food to eat, whereas the food in our house is known to be very good and Father Giovanni has often dined with us. Even after the troubles at the convent with my sister began to be whispered about. He is a good man. He has not judged us. He leaves that to God.

I think my father hopes that by giving this dinner to Father Giovanni and the Dominican clerks their hearts will be softened and they will intercede on his behalf with the Monsignor and with the Bishop if that would help. I think it is too late for that but I cannot tell him so. It would hurt him too much.

Esterina said my little sisters had wide-open mouths like the carp and she must take them inside to feed them. She said after that she was going to the prison with some food for my sister and for Giuditta. She would take them bread, olives, cheese, some oil and some dried fish, and some wine. She would take two baskets of food, one for my sister, and one for the guards, as a gift. My mother had given her leave to go. She had to go tonight, since she could not go tomorrow, it being a feast day and she needed here at home. She chattered on but I had not the heart to listen to her.

My father sat by the fire, very melancholy. He has not asked me to show

137

him this book. I think he does not want to read it. In his heart he knows now it can be of no use to him to study this record and examine all the evidence against my sister, in order to devise a plea to the Inquisitors to show her mercy. From time to time my mother passed near him and clapped him on the shoulder and told him all could still be well. She was going in and out of the kitchen and the room where we sat, very busy about the dinner for tomorrow. She said that she was going to light a fire in the oven in the bakehouse and get her dough risen in good time, so that she could be up early in the morning to cook it.

I have sat up to finish writing this. Even though I know I shall have to destroy a good part of it, yet it consoles me to write it. All the things I cannot tell my father and mother I have put down here. My thoughts are in prison like my sister is, yet they escape and run free as soon as I take my pen in my hand. I cannot make the words say only what I want. They have their own life and run across the page, to be free. Yet my thoughts are not free either. They are in prison with my sister and with Giuditta.

9 September

Now I know that I must destroy this writing I can put down in my book everything that has happened today. Then I shall make it disappear. I shall throw it into the fire and watch it burn. The Inquisitors cannot throw my sister and Giuditta into the fire and watch them burn. They have been prevented. They desired to do it but they were too late. Thanks be to Almighty God.

I accompanied my mother and father to Mass. Esterina stayed behind with the little girls, also to go on with the preparations for dinner. Father Giovanni, and Father Sebastiano and the other Dominicans, walked home with us afterwards. The Monsignor was gone with the Contessa, to keep her company and eat dinner elsewhere.

Father Sebastiano and I did not signal to each other by a single word or look that we knew each other before. It stays a secret, what we did together at night on the road. I think he has the same fear that I do, of its being found out, and his being disgraced and punished. I did not understand this before.

They all walked about the garden and the orchard with my father, discoursing on holy topics, while my mother and Esterina got the dinner. Then they came inside and looked at my father's books and talked to him about them. Then my father asked them questions about the sermon we had heard in church. So they explained it to him all over again. We ate dinner rather late, because of this holy conversation which went on so long. The Fathers were very hungry, for they had had nothing to eat that morning, and they had drunk a lot of wine while we were waiting for dinner. My father gave them his best wine. It stirs up the appetite and is very strong. My mother had prepared many dishes, which she sent in one or two at a time with Esterina, and then I served the Fathers their food. The best dish was a great plate of boiled meats, different ones all mixed together, eaten with a spiced *mostarda*. Later on we had the cakes my mother had baked this morning before going to church. Then all the Fathers fell asleep and slept for the rest of the afternoon, until it was evening. It was a hot day, and they had had only wine with which to quench their thirst. It being so delicious they had drunk a great deal of it. Then they woke up and went off to the church to say their Office.

I was in the garden and I saw that the door to the bakehouse was open. I went to close it, in case my mother had bread proving inside and the rats might get at it through the open door. Hearing a rustle, I went in. Two of the Dominicans were there, in the far corner. I saw their white habits and black scapulars and tonsured heads. Then I saw that in fact it was my sister Bona and Giuditta. Their faces were very white after so long in prison. Their eyes burned me. They stretched out their hands to forbid me to come closer. So I left them, and shut the door and locked it. I took the key in to my mother.

We sat down together and she told me it all. She sewed the habits with the cloth she got Esterina to buy. Last night she sent the habits into the prison in one of the baskets, depending on the guards being too eager to drink the wine she sent them to search the other basket. After the guard changed in the afternoon, Bona and Giuditta, dressed in their disguise, with their hoods pulled well down over their faces, got the new guard to let them out, which of course they did, thinking they were the Dominicans come as usual to pray over the heretics and now ready to go. They walked out and through the village to our house, while everyone was asleep in the hot afternoon, and hid in the bakehouse, which was always Bona's favourite place for hiding in when she was a child, so she knew to go there. My mother said that once it was discovered they were missing, no one would suspect us, for we had the priests here most of the day in holy conversation. And she thought the priests would not dare admit forgetting to send as usual two of their number to pray over the heretics in prison, for that would mean being found out that they were here asleep dead drunk for a large part of the day and were not engaged in edifying us by their example at all. She wept as she said this and said she hoped it would turn out to be as she thought but she could not be sure. I comforted her and we knelt together and said a prayer.

When I asked my mother why she was so sure my sister Bona was in such danger that she needed rescuing, she replied that while I was at the Inquiry each day with my father she had come into my room and taken out this book from where I had hidden it in my bedclothes and read what I had written the night before, so that she knew what was said at the Inquiry each day, whereas my father and I had tried to keep the proceedings a secret from her so that she would not be distressed.

I ran out very angry when she said this, at the thought of her reading all I wrote. I was ashamed she should see it, and understand all those things I meant to tell no one, least of all my father and herself. I came up here where I could be by myself with no one to see me.

Tomorrow at the Inquiry they would have questioned Bona, and the day after that they would have judged and condemned her to be burnt.

I heard the bolts on the back door of the garden scrape open then closed. That was Bona and Giuditta going out, into the darkness, to creep out of the village and begin their long journey south. I prayed to Santa Salome, the patroness of wandering women, that she would watch over them, protect and guide them and bring them to some safe place.

Today it was Father Sebastiano's turn, he told us on the walk back from church, to visit the two heretic women in prison. I think he must have wanted not to go, even with another Dominican by his side. He must not have wanted Bona and Giuditta to see him and be reminded of Sister Zita. He would have wanted to be invisible to them. I remember him as a man of great austerity in the matter of food and drink but no wonder this afternoon he preferred to take a lot of wine and then sleep.

My father has called up to me to come down and read to them in the room where they are sitting, from the book of chivalric romances the Contessa gave me when I left her house. He shouts up that they are too anxious and will not sleep and I must come down and join them.

Tomorrow, therefore, and not tonight, I shall burn this book. Now I will go and read my two dearly beloved parents a story about a beautiful maiden and her quest:

MARIE-JEANNE

We are but two but we speak as one. We share the words, some
in her mouth some in mine. Words wait, a store of them we
keep close and don't waste. We have no need of them for us,
most of the time. Our own talk does not use words. But you, sir. To talk to
you we will try to pick out some words you know, as rare as sweets on our
tongues. Lick them, then pass them out to you.

We will talk to you for one hour then you give us the cash, right? Two
hours, same deal. You hear our words, you take them, you pay for them.
We sell them to you at this price which is good for all of us, right?

This girl here with us? Our sweet girl she is. Our Eugénie de
Frottecoeur. She is in our tale too.

So. We were not born here, oh no. Some way back up north, we come
from. The north side of the Seine. A cold place for at least half the year, a
lot of fine rain, cold salt winds that blow in from the sea. Tall beech trees
hide the farms. Folk there are hard, tough. They have to be, to get through
life. We were born in a world of mud, wet, cold. Bed of straw in the room
next to the cows. In bed was the one warm place. Our warmth and our

smell was home. The sea was home too. Some way from our house, but we were glad to go there. Small deep roads led to it, a pass through cliffs and rock, then you fell down on to the beach. Like a birth. Cry of gulls, salt wind on your lips and fierce sun on your face, to walk there or just sit on the beach and stare at the sea, was bliss. We would like to go back just to see the sea once more. Not to our house. No point. But to the sea.

We talk too much, eh? You want us to stick to the point. What is the point? Oh, that. Yes. Right.

Well. It was like this. You could say, well Mum said so too, that when we wash our face and brush our hair we are fine and nice, we look good, skin with not one scar or spot, all our teeth, we are still young. Not yet two score years. Our hair, though, is the best thing. Most folk up there where we come from have blue eyes, and we do too, and fair hair, and we have that, but lots of it. Gold hair as fine as silk, a sort of gold floss, that drops to our waist. We comb it each night, wash it when we can, roll it up with a cap on top by day, twist it to two long plaits by night. Our gold crown. Proud of it, we are. Not a lot of girls have hair like that.

Hair to catch a man with. Our gold snare, he said. Our soft trap. Him the fast, keen bird, bold and brave, he saw us, flew up. We thought he caught us, but he said we caught him.

Times were hard at home. No spare pence to rub in the palm of your hand. Not much to eat. We were all so poor, there, in that small place. One man could not help the next. No food left to share, no cash to give. At night we drank. Thin sour stuff it was too. Kept the cold out though, we could dream a bit, made us less sad. Mum told a tale of the Queen, gold hair like ours, but a dress of cloth of gold, a new dress on each day, good hot food all the time, more than one huge house to live in, her whim was law to all.

Mum said she would take us to find more work. Leave Dad for a week or two, with the farm work, move close to the sea, find more work there. Mum did the wash for folk who had no time and could pay her. More folk like that near the sea, she thought. Wives of men who went out to sea to catch fish each day would be glad of help, she thought. A small town, more chance of work, more folk with cash. Some rich ones, too. One big house up on top of the cliff, two or three more in the town. Give it a try, she said. We found a room to rent, we got the work, we put by some cash to take home with us.

Then came the feast day. Near the end of March. A warmth in the air that meant spring. Mum did stay in our room, to sleep and rest. She said she felt sick and worn out, had a great need just to lie still. We said: we can't work, do the wash, it's a feast. We will go out, find some food for you, bring it home, don't fret so. All will be well, we said. Hand on mouth to hide the big smile. For a feast meant you could eat, drink, dance, play games, meet boys. With Mum at home we were more free. Wash and dry best skirt, the red one, coarse stuff but still our best, put on clean top and cap and sleeves, hair up like a great gold hill with small cap on top to show it off, shoes of wood on our nice small feet. Off to the *place*.

Here we met with all the rest, who came out of Mass and stood in great groups to chat and laugh, greet each one. We felt a bit shy at first. Not from round here. Our farm, half a day's walk to get there. Still, we know this place from when we are small kids and come in with Mum and Dad by cart, and we know it now from work. So then three, four girls greet us, say they have seen us do the wash down on the beach, say how are you, come with us and let's have some fun.

All the girls in one big group, all the boys next. Then a group of mums, a group of dads, all the old folk. We march off, with a song, a good tune to make you walk well, lift your feet. We take the steep path up the side of the cliff, to that green space in a bit from the edge, wide and flat. This is so high up, the top of the world it feels like. If you go to the edge and peer down, a sheer drop, great fear in us to feel that pull to fall off and fly yet we like it too and want to do it. This is where the great cliff arch jumps out to the sea and then goes down, a white chalk fall, to it. The curve of the arch is like a bridge, thin, as wide as a man. It leads to a small room of rock on top of the arch, you can just see it from the cliff, a round cave made in the rock. We would fear to go there, to fall off in mid-air then drown in the cold sea. We cry out to see it. The girls laugh at us. They tell us a tale of how once, a bad man took three girls there, did lock them up in the small rock room,

144

left them there to die. The girls sang hymns and sad songs all day and night, in a thin voice of gulls. Folk down in the town heard them. Then the three girls did turn to white gulls, flew out of the small hole in the wall of their rock room, flew off. Lost girls, they were, who did not come back. But at night, in spring, if you lie on the grass at the top of the cliff and keep still, you can hear them sing, that voice of a gull that cries and calls.

This tale made us sad, so to cheer up we did join in the dance. There was a tall bit of rock there, on the green, and we girls had to dance round it ten times, as a way to pray we could find a good boy to wed. We sang a song as we went round. Then there was the kind of dance we knew from home, when boys and girls, young and old, you all dance round in a ring to start with then twist round and dance up and down the lines in twos and skip first this way then that. We did love that dance. We did not want it to stop, with the good tune that made your feet jig and jump up to dance more and more. You get a stitch in your side, you sweat, you feel red in the face, but you don't care. You dance.

Some folk came out of the big house set back on the cliff. Rich folk with posh clothes and fine shoes. Three men in long wigs with curls, smart hats and coats. They stood at the edge of the green space, to watch us dance. We are not dumb, you know, sir. We knew they thought that what we did was a sport they could laugh at and mock if they chose, they saw it as a play we put on for them. So we held up our head, did kick our feet high, did our best, to try and scorn them, for we thought they should not laugh at our feast. At the end they gave us a clap.

All of us had to rest, get our breath back. So we had games then. We did play the one with nuts, do you know it? The girl holds them in her lap, with her skirt drawn on top, or in a bag, shut tight, a whole lot of them. The boys come up, pay two sous, have to guess, when they dip their hand in, if the nuts come out as odd ones or in twos. If the boy wins, if he is right, then she has to give him two score nuts. All the girls took part in this game, and we did too. A good way to meet boys. They stroll up, take a good look at you, choose to play or choose to walk off. A chance for you to get a good look at them, too. Start to make friends, if you like, if you want to. Your heart can stay light, you can laugh, flirt a bit, it's fun. The rules keep you safe, to start with. Then, the girls told me, if you like a boy and he likes you, you can join up in the dance, and then at night you might go for a walk. One of the girls gave us a share of her nuts, so that we could play with the rest.

One of the posh men with fine clothes came up to us, the young one, the one with the fair face and dark eyes. Bright gems stuck in the rings on his hands. He made a bow to us, said: may I play? He made the right guess when he brought out his fist full of nuts from our skirt lap, that they would add up odd. But we had no more nuts to give him as a prize, for he took them all that first time. We said so and he gave us a smile. He took a kiss from us. His cheeks were soft and smooth, not rough like our dad's face. He said would we take a walk with him, in some hours' time, when the dance and play were done for the day, when it was dark, and we said yes.

We told the girls, our new friends, that we would come back soon to join them, for the fun was not done yet, but we must go back down the cliff and see Mum, who was ill, and take her some food. They did cry to us to bring back some wood with us, for the great fire the boys would build once it grew dark. We brought Mum a pear in puff paste and a meat roll from one of the stalls set up in the *place*. She said she felt so sick still she could not eat it, so we had it for her, as well as the fresh crab we had bought as a treat. She drank some of the wine we gave her, then went back to sleep. We could not stay with her. It was too sad in this room, with the smell of her, hot and ill, in the air, a sort of stale breath. We stole out while she slept. We ran down to the beach, and caught up a great load of drift wood in our skirt, and took it back up the cliff.

The fire was built by the boys and lit by one of the girls. Each one threw on the wood he or she had brought. A huge pyre, so bright and so hot. We had to do a dance round it.

The posh young man came up to us. He said will you come for a walk? We said: a short one then, not too far from our friends. Just a quick one. His clothes were so fine, we were shy at first, and did not dare to look at him too much. But he was nice. He was shy too, and that put us at our ease.

He told us he did not live up here, in the big house, but in a great house down by the Seine. He had friends here, and had come to see them for the feast, but would have to go off next day and go back home, which made him sad, since he did like us so much. His name was a long one, hard to say. We called him *Love*. That made him laugh.

We were at the edge of the cliff now, in the dark. You could hear the sea, far down, the waves on the shore. We were near to the thin bridge of the top of the arch, that led to the room in the rock. The young man took us in his arms and did kiss us. Then he took off one of his rings, a big one with a bright-blue stone, and said: I dare you to walk with me out there, on the bridge, I dare you to cross the arch with me and go into the rock room, and I will give you this ring if you will come with me.

We said no, it would be wrong to go so far from our friends, and in the dark too. He did kiss us more, and said such sweet things to us. We got so hot from all this, as though we were too close to the great fire we had just left, his hands on us, on our face and neck, made us feel a flame in us, and we did like him so much, and we did want the ring, so we said yes, and we ran to the bridge, in great fear, took a deep breath, went hop skip run and got to the end and so got to the small room cut in the rock on the top of the arch.

When we were there it was all right. It was just us with him. In the dark we could not see much but we could feel, and we could speak. He took our cap off and made us let down our hair and he hung on to it like two thick ropes. Well sir, we are sure you know the rest. We do not need to tell you what went on then. We did like it, though he was so quick, we did want yet more. We could not feel it was such a great sin as the priests all say, for it was so sweet and hot. Then we went back, but he did not give us the ring, but went off. I think the girls had seen what he did or at least where we went, for they gave us stern looks and one or two shook their heads at us and some did laugh. We went back down the cliff, to the room in the town, where Mum still slept, and went to bed. So she did not know we had been out so late, nor what we had done.

We went to find him. We left Mum and went off. We told her, and it was part of the truth if not all, that we had to go to find more work, to get cash for her and Dad and us.

We went on foot, of course. Two days' walk, no more. The road goes down the side of the Seine, it was not hard to see the huge, grand house he had told us of. We got maid work there. Ask at the back door, yes, do come in, sure there is work, you can wash shirts and sheets, good. So we wait, and hope to see him.

But he had a wife. We saw them walk out, slow, on the grass, arm in arm. She was young and fair, with rich clothes all in pale blue silk, her shoes too. But she was a bit too thin and pale. Her mouth had a most firm set to it, though she was so young. He bent his lips to her hand, odd we thought, for us he did kiss most on the mouth. She was such a posh girl, that one. One kiss on the hand and she went all pink. He gave her a smile and a bow, then he strode off. The maids told us he had gone back to see the King and Queen, dance all night and ride in the park and hunt, all that kind of thing. Eat off gold plates, loll in soft chairs, stay in bed till noon. This maid said: they grind the face of the poor! Why are we so poor? They are too rich, that's why. Look at the huge tax poor folk have to pay. She went on and on, but we did not hear much. We thought of him. He had not seen us. We stood on the far side of the hedge, a small hole to peep through. We were sad. But we thought well, he will come back soon. He might see us next time. And at least here there is food, a place to sleep, a dole of coins each month to save for Mum and Dad. The posh girl, once he was gone, was the boss of the house. She made us pray morn, noon and night, which we did not like too much, and we had to go to Mass each week, but it could have been worse.

The posh girl would have a child in six months' time. We knew this, for no more red cloths and rags came to the wash each month. And she was so thin, you could see her swell. We saw her walk in the park, with a book, and we saw her in church. But the odd thing was, we too had a stop of blood, no more red cloths that month nor the next. We got big. The maids found out. How could they not? We got thrown out. We were *bad*. Such a *bad* sin.

They would not just let us go. We could have tried to go home, tried to get Mum to take us back in, tell us we were bad, yes, but still there was love in her heart for us. We don't know, that might have been true, but it might not, she might have been so cross that she too threw us out. But there we were, put in this house like a jail, run by nuns, with a lot of girls in the same state as us, big but not wed and no chance of it. It was run to the posh girl's plan, to save our souls the nuns said. They took our small bit of cash off us when we were put in, to pay for our food and bed they said. They made us work, work, work. And pray, pray, pray. It was like hell, that place. Bad food, cold, such a strict rule, worse than jail. Now we loathe nuns so much we can't tell you. This lot felt hate for us, hate for sex, hate for the babes we would bear. One or two of them did try to be good to us now and then, but not much. Once a week the priest came in to talk to us, on sin and hell most of the time, but he was too old, too weak, the nuns did not let him come close to us, he could not help us. I think he had a bit of love in his heart for us, for how we felt. Once he said to us: poor child, dear child. But that was it. Not much good to us, was it?

When the time came for the babe to be born, that was bad too. Put in a small room like a cell, left all on your own for hours and hours, with pain like a mad dog that tears you up. Such fear, of this pain, and then that it got worse, and we cried out and the nuns did not come. We cried out for Mum and she was not there. The nuns came in on day two, right at the end, to get the child born, make the sign of the cross on it, make it a child of God not our child. To be left on your own like that, in such pain, for so long. That was the real sin if you ask us. Our fear was part of the pain. Now we have no fear left. The nuns took care of that.

So. Skip a lot of the next bit. You do not need to know it. You do want to hear? Well. That was the time when we found we were two. Not the child. Not her. We mean *us*. We had a friend now. There is the Mad Dog girl, and the Rock girl. We found we were two in that small room in the nuns' jail, just as the child got born. We tore in two. That made it not quite so bad. The child was a girl. As soon as they could, the nuns took her from us. They put her with the rest of the babes, to be all in the same place, far from their bad mums. They said to us: get on with your work now and get your strength back, then you can go back in the world and get a job and be good, bind up your tits, no leak of milk please, here is a cloth, look sharp.

They had cut our hair off when we gave birth, to make sure we were clean they said, no lice or nits. But we are sure those nuns just did it to make us feel as bad as they could. We lost our hair, all that great soft gold mass of it, our crown. But we kept it. The nuns cut off our plaits and let them drop on the floor, then the bell rang and they had to run off and pray with the rest. So we took the plaits and hid them in our bed and kept them. We had one plait each, one for the Mad Dog girl and one for the Rock girl. But at the point when we lost the child, when the nuns took her off and that was it no more child 'bye 'bye, we made a pact, each to each. We would stay friends and we would stay true. One would not run off and leave. As a sign of this pact, we wove the two plaits to make one. One thick, long tress. We held it in our arms and sang a quick song to it then hid it in the bed. At night we held it. Our own hair grew back a bit. A few curls this time, but thin, short.

Tires us out to talk so much. A drink now, that would help. Wet our dry throat. Thanks.

Soon we had to leave that hell hole, that nuns' jail. The posh girl had had her child, we were told, a girl. On the day she was born, we got more bread on our plates and a sip or two of thin wine. The bells rang, the nuns were full of joy, though it was a girl and not a male heir. They told us the name they gave her. Eugénie they said it was. A posh name for a posh child. What did we care? That high bleat, so shrill, of the nuns, their bad food and cold house, we were well rid of all of it.

We went home. But Mum and Dad were gone. Thrown out, for they had not paid their tax or their rent for some months. The Rock girl would not let us sit down and cry. New folk in our old home, so what. Get back on the road, start the hunt for work.

We thought we knew hard times, but these were worse. I do not think, sir, you can know. To feel so cold, have not much to eat, your clothes stiff with dirt, dust and grime deep in your skin and hair, no walls of a house round you to keep you safe at night, no roof to keep you dry. You live in the rain. Wet through. Youth gone. Lack of joy. Lack of hope. Though at night we saw our child, with her crown of gold hair in a thick high plait on top of her head, as ours used to be, and blue silk shoes on her feet and a clean dress. This way we knew the look of her, how she was as she grew up. Sad for her not to know her mum, though. But at least she came to see us at night. At night Mad Dog girl and Rock girl slept in the same bed, arms and legs in a tight knot. Tied each to each by that gold plait of hair. When we woke from such a dream, of the child, Mad Dog would cry a bit but Rock would shout: no you don't, don't you dare cry.

Few jobs at the time. Not much work. To live was to starve. We were two old girls on the road. Two old hags! We bought and sold old things as we went by, to make a bit of cash to buy some food with. Tried to sleep in barns, that kind of thing. The bark and bite of farm dogs, we have a great fear of that now. A dog like that finds you, he tries to bite you.

What did we sell, sir? We sold *us*, sir, we sold our clothes, we sold sticks to start fires with. We sold us as much as we could, best thing we had to sell. It was sad the day we had to sell the red skirt, last fine thing we had on our back. Still. What else could we do?

Two score years we spent on the road. We did not die. By some luck or chance we keep our lives, though these feel so thin and light, as though they hang by one thread and each day it might be cut.

By now we have crossed the Seine, come south a bit. Some kind of a war on, that is all we know, we duck out of the way as much as we can. We hear that the King and Queen and most of that lot have been thrown in jail. Good, we think: let them find out what it is like, it is their turn. Hope the nuns are in there with them, that's all! But we still lack food, still have to sleep out, hedge or barn, see what turns up each night, so this news makes us shrug a bit. We shall see, we say. Life stays harsh for us. We are tramps and whores and that's as low as you can get, right? No change in our life, that is for sure. At least not yet.

We get as far as the Loire, and stop. For there was a fair on, in that town we came to, just the thing for us. Buy a bit, sell a bit, spot the odd chance

151

to make some cash, keep our wits about us. That day, our old life came to an end and we saw the start of a new one. If there was a God we would bless Him.

The fair was some small way out of town, by the side of the great stream. Tents and stalls each way you look and one big space left clear for folk to play. You know the kind of thing. Pay two sous and stone a cock to death, pay two more sous and break the neck of a live goose with thick sticks, the goose strung up by a cord from a tree. Climb up a grease pole to win a prize, or join in a sack race or a pig race. All the things folk love to do. You could have your sore tooth drawn, if you felt brave, or your warts made to go with a pray-cum-spell, you could play cards or bowls, you could drink a great deal. Most people there did that, and we did too. It was a spring day, but chill. We love drink, it makes us warm. We went up and down, had a good look at all the stalls. One was like a small stage on wheels, with a play put on of the King and Queen. When their heads fell off the boys took them to play football with. They had two teams: the wed and the ones not wed. A girl who had just got wed, the week past, threw the ball in, and off they went.

There was more to see in the fair than that. If you paid two sous, you could look at a cage with a were wolf in it, a she-wolf. Teeth like pearls, much paint on the lips and cheeks, hands like claws, long black hair in curls like a wig. More like a witch than a wolf, we thought, and we were sure her tail was a false one, just sewn on to the hem of her skirt. What a rant and a wail she made. She was a real old hag we thought, worse than us! In the cage next to her was a girl in a blue dress who sat still on the ground like a sad beast, her eyes cast down. She made a noise like a bird, a thin plaint like a gull.

Then we knew. She was our lost girl. The one the nuns took from us, whom we had not seen for two score years. But we knew she was ours. For a start, her hair. Long and gold, a flow of it down her back like ours had been once. Her eyes, blue as ours. We were sure of who she was. But she would not look at us when we spoke soft words to her through the bars of the cage. She kept her head down and she sang her sad gull song just for her own ears.

The man who kept her said she was mad and deaf and dumb. A mad posh girl made a good show, he thought. How come, posh? we said. He said he found her in the Frottecoeur house, when it was set fire to a year back, and he and a whole gang of men went in, once the flames were high, to take what they could from those bad rich folk. He spat on the ground at this point. She does not look too posh to us, we said. Look at her big ring with blue glass in it, he said, look at all that silk on her back, tell me that's not posh!

A ring with a blue stone in it. We saw one like it once, a long time back. *He* said he would give it to us. He our love. But did not. And we knew silk when we saw it. But still we felt sure this must be our girl. We waited for her for so long. We said to ourself: keep cool, think of a plan, how you can play a trick on this man and steal her from him. We said to him: and the old wolf girl, is she from the same house? Yes, he said: the old bag, I was kind, I took them home with me, I could have left them to die there, but I took care of them, none can say I did not, I led them out through the smoke and fire when all the rest in there were dead. Burnt up, to white ash. No bones left. Nought to put in the graves. None knows these two still live and bring me in cash. God knows they and their like stole the cash from all of us for so long!

We came back to the fair, and back to this man, when it grew dark and much of the fair was shut, the mouths of tents sewn up, the flaps of stalls lace down. We brought drink with us, and gave the man some and drank with him. We said: do you want one more wolf? We have a wolf to show you, a real she-wolf. Then Mad Dog girl lifts the skirt, and Rock girl stares at him with eyes so cool but full of sex, and he says yes, sure, I like your wolf, let's do it. For free, we say: as a gift, for we like you. So we do it with him, round the back of the cage, on the ground in the dark, for as long as we can, so that when he does come it's a huge come, and he falls to a sleep like a swoon. Quick. Take the cage keys from him while he sleeps. Find our girl in her cage, and join her there. Lock the door on us, throw the keys far out through the bars. Lost keys. Found girl.

In here, you see, it is dry, it is warm in all this straw, walls and a roof to

153

keep you safe, bars to see through. But best of all, of course, she is here too. Our Eugénie. She is not lost but found. She is still shy of us, shy to talk and speak. But not mad. She knows us, for one thing. She loves us. We give her the plait of our hair we have kept with us all these years on the road, and she holds it in her arms and sings to it. She sings: mum mum mum mum mum. You can hear her, yes?

Sir, you have the look of a kind and good man, though you are a priest. You say you would like to help us. Sir, you paid the man your two sous to come and see us, we know, but you did say to us too that you would pay us for our tale of who we are and how we got here. Please give us the cash now. To buy new red skirts for all of us. Then if you like, if you have some more cash to spare, we will tell you one more tale. This one, we swear, is the real truth. There are two of us, you see. So there are two tales. Here is the next one:

GEORGINA

Next, I imagine that the signature G. Mannot, in the bottom right-hand corner of these canvases, a flourish in black paint, the letters wide and curved, indicated her ambivalence, her wish for secrecy and her love of disguises. I'm sure that G. could point to either George or Georgina, both George and Georgina, even as it concealed them.

(close-up of signature)

She embarked upon a daring masquerade, like something in one of the modern novels we know she read and loved, in which she

(photomontage of *flâneurs/flâneuses* by the Seine
the stalls of the *bouquinistes*
novels with yellow covers)

allowed herself two selves, two lives, or was it three? Her life as a woman in London, her life as a man in France, his/her experience at the moment of crossing over from one to the other and back again.

(presenter talking to camera
in the exhibition hall
Mannot's paintings clearly visible in the background)

How did she do it exactly? How did she get away with it for so long? Perhaps I should say *he*. I can't say *shehe*.

(put montage in here? – photographs of the period, e.g. the mass-produced pornographic pics of women, pics of men half-nude doing wrestling & gymnastics, etc.)

Two bodies, apparently separate and different, male and female, which were joined together by the to-ing and fro-ing between them. One skin stitched to the other then ripped off, over and over again. Two separate land masses, one called England and one called France, which were con-nected by the sea drawing itself back and forth, back and forth, between them. Her parents: a French man and an English woman, with the Channel between them, with the sea (herself in those waters?) held in their arms. She made herself into a marriage. She married two split parts of herself, drew them together and joined them, and she also let each one flourish individually.

(close-up of one of the pictures – perhaps *Night Steamer*?)

How did she do it? What was the process involved? The paintings reveal her gestures with the brush, record the traces left by her hand, the way she worked the paint on to the canvas. But I'm not at all sure how she made herself, first into a woman and then into a man. Nor how she learned to change so fast from one style to the other.

I can only surmise about George-Georgina, for the changeover was performed out of sight, in darkness, in the middle of the night, on the cross-Channel steamer. Georgina Mannot got on to the boat, and George Mannot disembarked on the other side.

(presenter to camera)

Other films in this series on G. Mannot's work will consider the paintings themselves, their place in the history of art, their relationship to late-nineteenth-century French and English painting. Tonight's film offers moments in a fantasized biography of Mannot. It doesn't attempt to tell the truth. We shall circle around a single, and perhaps the most sensational, aspect of Mannot's life, which has long overshadowed the serious evaluation of her painting: her forays into drag. Our film tonight suggests a possible scenario. One more illusion of reality.

(close-up of *The Travelling Bag*)

Her truth was a trick performed in the darkness of the Ladies' Cabin of the overnight boat to France. Imagine Georgina undressing, her rapid fingers unbuttoning her white blouse and navy-blue skirt, rolling them up and stuffing them into her canvas bag. Her heavy dark-blue traveling coat, big and severely cut, might earn her a few raised eyebrows as she stepped up the companionway in England, her skirts bunched in one gloved hand, but in France, when she disembarked, it was a man's coat, worn by a shabby painter, and attracted not one glance.

In the darkness Georgina pulled on a shirt and waist-coat, tucked the shirt into her trousers, yanked up her braces, slipped her feet into a pair of boy's boots. Slicked back her hair with macassar oil, twisted it into a small tight bun, stuck a cap on her head. Hands delved into pockets, shoulders shifted experimentally from side to side. Such pleasure to feel the cloth of the trousers tight across her pelvis, over her hips. To be held in by trousers was to be both caressed and confined. Trousers outlined her shape and gave her back herself.

157

(close-up of *The Fisherman's Son*)

Her tall lean body that was George. When morning came it was George who sauntered up and down the deck, yawning in the salty air, who leaned indolently against the rail to gaze at the bustle in the port.

(close-up of *The Quayside at Le Havre*)

George hoisted his bag, strolled down the companionway. One ordinary English spinster more or less: nobody was counting, nobody missed her. And George was just the young English fellow leaving the boat.

(close-up of *Self-Portrait*)

In the *Self-Portrait* that opens this exhibition, the painter stares out at us, bold, amused, a little sly. In one hand she hoists her palette, in the other a bunch of brushes. Her hair, which seems to be cut short and brushed severely back, is perhaps confined in a bun behind her head that we can't see. Her painter's smock is baggy and loose, of indeterminate gender. Yet we see her as a woman because in England, though she signed herself simply G. Mannot, she was known as a woman painter, with all that that implied at the time in terms of her special sensibility and special, restricted, place. In this self-portrait she has chosen to transport herself from the studio to the foyer of the Hôtel au Rendezvous des Artistes in Etretat, where we know she stayed during successive summers in the 1880s. A hotel that was designed to look ancient yet was of course a modern fake, born of the craze for all things medieval at the time. Here, the painter has chosen to include details of the carved interior: a cat pawing a mouse; a snake; a butterfly; on what looks like part of a balustrade.

(close-up of *Hôtel au Rendezvous des Artistes, Etretat — façade*)

Part of Georgina's façade as George, we know from contemporary memoirs of the painter, was to tell contradictory stories of her childhood. We know surprisingly few of the facts. We are told that her father, Jean, first crossed the Channel when he was no bigger than a pearl, cradled in fluid, inside his mother's body. The widow, a Frenchwoman from Paris, gave birth to her son in London, where he grew up. She became a dress-maker to the ladies of Kensington, who liked having a Parisienne to run up their frocks. Baby Jean played with wooden bobbins and cotton reels on the floor of the workshop where the sewing-machines clacked and the three apprentices ground out seam after seam.

    (close-up of *The Fitting*
           Model Resting)
           The Dressmakers at Work)

Jean grew up among women's skirts, amongst an abundance of dresses. He liked the stuffy workshop, where he could stroke lengths of silk and satin, wind net veiling around himself, pass ostrich feather across his cheeks and mouth. He was king baby all right, sole adored fledgling in a nest of mother birds who carried fat worms to his beak and sang to him to keep his night terrors away.

    (close-up of *Cutting out the Pattern*
           The Pinking Shears)

Consolation came in the form of a strip of suede he pulled rhythmically in and out between his bare toes, snipped fragments of beaded ribbon he pinched between his fingertips like sugar grains, scraps of cotton lace he could poke his thumbs through. He was his mother's cherub, and she dressed him in angel-frocks, frilled and sashed, which he dirtied with his floor forays.

    (close-up of *Mother and Child*
           Boys in Kensington Gardens
           The Boating Pond)

When he was five his hair was cut and he was born into boyhood, into the touch of leather, the cold and hard strap that belted his trousers made of black serge that scratched, the rigid shiny straw of boaters, the cool glaze of the ribbon encircling the brim, the stiff wool of stockings, the constraints of buttoned gaiters, of laced boots.

Jean was apprenticed to the clothes trade in Paris. On his return to London he took over his mother's business, and he met Gladys and married her.

(close-up of *Madame Mannot at the Window*
montage here perhaps of photos from the Mannot family album, e.g. Jean and Gladys on their wedding day, Gladys as a young girl, Gladys with a tennis racquet, in archery costume, driving the dog-cart, etc.)

I think Georgina Mannot tried to paint tactile and sensuous experience. For example, the experience of lovemaking, of touching another. She was obsessed with painting surfaces that appear both hard and soft, that seem about to give way, to collapse, that gleam seductively, that suggest enclosure, wrapping . . .

(close-ups of *The Egg Stone*
  Pebbles at Etretat — Low Tide
  The Unmade Bed
  Still Life — Oysters
  The Negligée)

I think that in order to find out who and what she was she tried to imagine her parents making love, making her. She invented a wedding night, dreamed how Jean laid Gladys bare, divested of her heavy nightdress wrappings. He embraced her body warm and deep as velvet smooth as silk, he grasped her skin as though it were one more layer of satiny material he could lift off. Released from her stays and corsets and buckles and belts Gladys was voluptuous, bales of flesh that unrolled for him and enclosed him, he put her on like a fur coat over his nakedness and luxuriated in her, he discovered her silk and velvet insides with grunts of pleasure while Gladys flowed about him, sturdy and soft, a warm fleshy sea that picked him up, little boat, her pearl of a man, tossed him up and down, kept him from drowning.

(close-ups of *Washerwomen on the Beach, Etretat*
                        The Wet Sheets
                        The Linen Cupboard)

They tumbled about in the bed, sank into and on to each other, rampaged happily. Their words got mixed up, they lost their names in each other, they was a creature with four arms and four legs, a cunt wrapping itself around a swollen prick, thick lips swallowing a thick tongue,

(close-ups of *Sunrise* – the series, 1–4)

Glean, Jad, Gladjean, they grew hotter and cried out and pressed down and wet each other and frowned and groaned then at last slept, big arms folded around each other. Jean, who was so close to his mother, found her again in Gladys. He made all his wife's clothes, and also those for his daughter Georgina.

(montage of photos of Georgina as a baby, a child, a small girl, with her parents, etc.)

Her parents allowed Georgina to train at the Slade as a painter. They indulged her in her desire, as though she had demanded to be sent to finishing school. They did not expect her to become a professional.

Georgina moved into cheap lodgings in Russell Square. By day she painted. By night she walked around the city. She cut her hair. She trimmed it even further, later on, so that she could go bare-headed as a man in France. In England, as a woman influenced by the movement for

161

dress reform, she abandoned the fashionable clothes her father loved to have made for her, which constrained and emphasized her breasts and waist, her stomach and hips, which required corsets and stays and tight bodices. She chose loose clothes in muslin and linen and chintz, she liked overalls and smocks, wraps that she could fling on and off in a second. Her father scoffed at this greenery-yallery artiness, at this need for clothes to be comfortable.

(close-up of *Odalisque in Kensington*)

Georgina sometimes wore trousers. Black velvet ones, baggy, gathered at the ankle. With them went a little embroidered jacket, short-waisted, cut generously enough that she could move her arms easily, in fact forget altogether what she was wearing as she lounged in an armchair smoking a Turkish cigarette, one leg dangling over the arm, slippered foot gently waving to and fro, the other leg stretched out in front of her.

Dressing as a man was almost simply an extension of how she dressed every day as a student painter. We know that she first experimented with cross-dressing during her stay in Paris, after she left the Slade. Like George Sand before her, she found that men's clothes meant that she was not accosted when she roamed around by herself at night. I think she loved the risk and adventure involved in appearing to be what she was not. I think she enjoyed the fun of the different, the forbidden.

(close-up of *The Cliffs at Etretat*
       Bar des Etrangers, Etretat)

During her working summers in Etretat she could now become part of the masculine group of painters who met together in the evenings to drink and smoke, play cards, argue. Nobody felt obliged to treat her differently, put her in her place by praising her appropriately delicate touch and suitably feminine subject matter, by offering her advice and help she had not asked for. She could tip back her chair, crack jokes, smoke cigarettes, eat and

162

drink what she liked, and advance strong opinions, and nobody thought any the worse of her. There were a great many women painters in France at the time, but Georgina does not appear to have made friends with any of them. Perhaps she preferred her disguise, the *entrée* it gave her into the masculine world she admired as superior. Perhaps she feared being pulled into a feminine world of painting she had been taught to label inferior.

She *looked* at women a great deal, however, with a gaze that searched, penetrated, caressed. Over and over again her brush re-created the surface of the skin of women's bodies and faces. Flesh, warm and living and alluring, is one of her major subjects. Clothes and skin. The texture of materials is always present, compares to that of flesh.

(close-ups of *Cauchoise Girls in their Sunday Attire*
        The Cook at the Hôtel au Rendezvous des Artistes, Etretat
        The Bath
        Picnic in the Orchard
        Young Woman Asleep)

Three female faces in particular come back again and again in the paintings. They return like ghosts. They seem to have haunted Georgina. First of all – Hermine Patelin, Georgina's sometime landlady. She sketched her obsessively, in a compulsively modern series.

(close-ups of *Hermine Ironing* – the series, 1–6; drawings
        Hermine Seated by the Window – the series, 1–6; drawings
        Hermine Digging Potatoes – the series, 1–6; drawings
        Hermine Chopping Leeks – the series, 1–6; drawings)

Secondly there is the series of studies of Félicité Latouche, niece of the *patronne* of the *Hôtel au Rendezvous des Artistes*, who took over, with her husband, the running of the hotel in the late 1880s. Besides the declared portraits of Félicité –

(close-ups of *Félicité Seated on the Bed* – drawing
Félicité Eating Greengages – drawing
Félicité Wrapped in a Mantle – drawing)

– her image turns up unnamed in many of the paintings done at the time.

(close-ups of *Washerwomen on the Beach, Etretat*
Picnic in the Orchard
Young Woman Asleep
Fishing Nets on the Beach, Etretat
On the Promenade, Etretat)

Did George/Georgina look at Hermine and Félicité as mirrors, or as other to herself/himself? Certainly the themes of reflecting surfaces – tin mugs, silvery zinc bars in cafés, looking-glasses, windowpanes, silk panels on screens – recur constantly in the work, always in conjunction with female flesh. As a child Georgina sat on the fur rug in her mother's bedroom and watched Gladys dress and undress, try on hats, hoist her breasts up to the edge of her *décolletage* and settle them just behind their whalebone wall. She watched her father pin and tuck the dress her mother wore as regally as any model in the dress-shop *salon*, adjust it to hang exactly right, to drag its weight of satin bunched folds along the floor with just the right amount of resistance. The material spoke the body, its yielding, its reluctance, and the woman was completed within the gilt frame of the long mirror. Face and arms took on a second skin of scented powder. Silken legs were stroked by the child before her hand was shrugged away. An evening dress of pale-pink satin, with cream and dark ivory shot lights in its folds. Georgina painted her mother throughout her life, from the vantage point of that child crouched in the corner stretching out her hand, in a series of paintings

(close-ups of *Nude Woman Reclining* – the series, 1–10)

which celebrate her mother's body in full bloom and then in middle and in old age, and which perhaps take their revenge on that mother, who pushed her daughter's hand away and went out dancing, by fixing her in paint, by representing her as eternally present. In these paintings the flesh of the model (whose calmly confronting gaze is certainly that of Gladys herself) takes up almost all the pictorial space so that we practically rub our noses in it when we get close up to look at the manipulation of the paint. Yet at the same time the rules of the gallery, like those of the mother, say Don't Touch. We are attracted, seduced, forbidden, by this fecund and abundant body made newly available to us, unwrapped from the silky sheets of the bed, just as we are separated from it by the edge of the canvas and the painting's frame. The cream-coloured silk sheets, flung back, reveal Gladys's pink and cream body, like petals torn from a rose to display its heart. Can you remember the sound of ripping silk? In the workroom the dressmaker's scissors slithered through the thin material, cutting and tearing. Did the child Georgina imagine lifting off her mother's skin, wrapping herself in it, stealing it for herself like a cloak discarded by the mother who goes away to dance? Was Jean allowed to lift the corner of that pink silk skin and creep inside where she, the angry daughter, was now forbidden to go? Was it only Jean who could design the way that skins should be stitched together to make the mother's beautiful coat? When the child flopped awkwardly on to her mother's lap Gladys pushed her off again: don't be silly, you're much too old for cuddling, look, you're creasing my new dress. Yet Gladys consented to sit, over and over again, for that series of portraits painted by her daughter. She allowed her daughter's gaze. Perhaps she enjoyed it. Jean had told her, over and over, how beautiful she was. Perhaps she liked being watched, perhaps she liked letting her daughter discover her, make her up. The caress of the eyes she did permit. She would have made a good striptease artist, that lovely and tantalizing Gladys.

(close-up of *The Basket of Chestnuts*)

Georgina, who considered herself not beautiful at all as a woman, surprised everybody by marrying, in her mid-forties, her lover, the painter Clement Last, whom she had first met at the Slade twenty-five years before. Clem wrote to a friend describing their walk together in Richmond Park in October, how they picked up fallen chestnuts, holding them gingerly by a single spine then tossing them into Clem's greatcoat pockets; how, split open, the cases showed their satiny white insides in which nested the black nuts exactly fitting together. What he did not go on to say was how they returned to Georgina's tiny house (she was living near the Angel now, in Moon Street) and made love on the floor of her studio under the big attic skylight, lying on the white fur rug inherited from her mother.

(close-ups of *Male Nude Reclining* – the series, 1–10; drawings)

Georgina unpeeled Clem like a fruit, she laid him bare to her gaze, her hungry eyes looking and looking, oh you're a nice bit of flesh you are she murmured, biting his big white shoulder gently, it was the colour of milk and tasted sweet, of Clem's own particular mix of sweat and hay and oranges. He was like a chestnut on the outside, all prickles, unshaven, her bristly bride she told him laughing, but inside he was white fur, glossy and new, like satin. She cracked him open, she split him, her tongue darted in and licked him, her soft red chisel to part his casing and reach his insides, she undid him slowly and carefully like a present. Both naked on the white rug. Like two pigs rooting for truffles, cavorting, fat and white-skinned, full of juice, snorting and kicking up their heels, as fair as milk.

(close-up of *Hermine Skimming the Milk*)

Georgina encircled Clem's cock with her hand, she drew the ring of her fingers up and down. Like watching the stem of a flower come to life, a thick white stem full of sap. She pinned him down on the white fur rug, by spreading her arms and legs along his. She arranged him to her liking, arms out, legs apart. She knelt over him and nuzzled him, kissed her way slowly down his stomach, licked his navel well, rasped her tongue into his

166

hair, then she seized his cock between her lips like a titbit and pretended to swallow it over and over again. He lay back trustingly, he abandoned himself to her teeth seizing him very gently, he seemed to have no fear she would bite him too hard, he was in her power, smiling up at her. She licked his cock round and round then engulfed it again in her mouth letting her tongue play over him at the same time as her lips slipped back and forth over and around him. Where did you learn to do this? Clem shouted delightedly and she let go her mouth from his cock for a second almost choking with laughter and shouted back: at my mother's breast of course where else; and he was magically turned into Gladys, her big white body, and he was a plump white cocky breast at which she sucked her fill, as long as she wanted, and he was Clem lying back fists curled up calling come and fuck me come and fuck me. Georgina's cunt was streaming wet, it was open wide and fat and slippery with the delight of her other mouth sucking, she sat on Clem and rode him up and down. Then later on they roasted and ate the chestnuts, Georgina full of Clem's milk which he gave to her as much as she wanted. A drop fallen on the rug. She put her finger to it and licked, to know what it tasted like. Sweetsaltsour. The white milk of chestnuts.

(close-up of *Night Steamer*)

Heavily pregnant, Georgina departed on honeymoon with Clem. It is thought that up to this point Mannot's friends around Etretat still knew him/her only as a man. I try to imagine their reaction and I fail. Clem in a letter to a friend recorded how they stayed at the *Hôtel au Rendezvous des Artistes*. The patronne, Félicité Latouche, herself made up their bed, and insisted on giving them the best linen sheets from her trousseau to sleep in. This affected Georgina very deeply, Clem wrote. She had not dreamed of receiving such kindness from Félicité.

(presenter to camera)

In fact, Hermine Patelin, who dictated her memoir of Georgina to Madame Latouche, who kept it among her papers, where it was discovered after her death, insisted that she knew all along of Georgina's masquerade as George. One hot afternoon, Hermine claimed she came across the young painter bathing in the stream that ran behind her farmhouse, and recognized that *he* was clearly a *she*. All white and smooth as an egg, she said: a goose who changed into a swan and back again! Hermine was intrigued by her discovery. She hid Georgina's feminine clothes for her in a special cupboard, behind a pile of sheets, and she washed her monthly rags for her, hanging them to dry in a disused room so that they should not be seen.

(close-up of *The Secret*)

In return Georgina gave Madame Patelin a picture, whose whereabouts are today unknown. In her memoir of Georgina's life with her, Hermine Patelin says of this picture:

168

LOUISE

I gave her a name but I did not know her. She hid herself in a dream world. In my opinion. She wasn't mine. I mean she kept herself close. Getting a word from her was like prising open an oyster shell. You know those short-bladed knives, wide and small, that they use?

Oysters are slimy and cold. They taste of lemon, salt, the sea. Like little dead tongues. The first time I tasted one I spat it out. You can cut yourself on the frilled edges of the shells, they are so sharp.

So many disappointments in my life. So many caresses yearned for but not received.

My daughter lowered her eyelids and looked away when I spoke to her. She twisted her lips, then pressed them together. Sealed shut. She spread

169

her fingers across her face, a curtain of skin. Who's got your tongue? I would call: cat got your tongue? Who cut it out eh?

Those caresses my husband couldn't give, he wouldn't learn, couldn't hear me when I asked, he forgot each time my desire for caresses, just jumped in so nervous and quick, after a few years I gave up asking him to caress me, I stopped my mouth with a stone.

Frederica, we called her in the beginning. Then we shortened it to Freddy, bit too much of a mouthful otherwise. She was a lovely baby, and so good.

We gave her everything a child should have: food clothes a roof over her head a good education. But it wasn't enough. There was something else she wanted. I never knew what it was. She made me feel so terrible for not giving it to her. But how could I give it to her when I didn't know what it was? What she gave to me was reproaches. Suffering.

She was very difficult. When I was young I wasn't like that. I didn't cause my parents such pain and worry. I never behaved as she has. Why did she have to? I grew up all right. Why couldn't she?

I did my best. What more could I do? But for her it wasn't enough. She blamed me. She hurt me so much. Shouting terrible things, treating me like her enemy. Shouting about sex. She became a different person. Not our daughter any more. She went out of control. I was afraid she was mad. She was trying to kill me with how she behaved.

Tarty, the word the neighbours used. How I suffered, knowing what my husband suffered, having a daughter who behaved like that.

She said she wanted to go to art school, like her friend Martin, she said she wanted to make films about art. She threw away all our hopes for her. She wouldn't listen to what I said. Just shouted at me. Wicked and evil things. She was evil, to say what she said to me. That I hadn't loved her properly.

Just before her eighteenth birthday she left. She didn't take much with her. But, something horrible, she had cut all her hair off, her thick plait, and left it hung over the mirror for me to find.

It was the kind of thing she would do. She'd always done things like that with bits of hair and I don't know what, she thought it was a game, she said it was some kind of art. I thought it was cruel of her, she did it to hurt me.

Anger is the stone in my heart that I have carried since childhood, the stone I must not throw, let my daughter carry it for me, let her clasp the stone and let my heart be lightened.

I emptied the rubbish from her room. The old broken toys and so on I put in the dustbin, and the plait of hair, and her clothes. When both dustbins were full, I put carrier bags by the side, papers spilling over from the tops.

The dustmen came on a Tuesday, and this was a Friday. Such a mess those dustbins looked, papers blowing about. I didn't like the look of them at all. Enough mess in our street, what with dogs' dirt and all the sweet wrappers and crisp packets the schoolchildren drop. So, in the end, when I couldn't stand the sight of all that rubbish any more, I took the carrier bags back into the house. To wait for Tuesday, when the dustmen came round and I could put out proper black plastic sacks.

Papers and notebooks, drawings, sketches. I had a quick look, to see if there was anything that should really be kept, in case Freddy came back and wanted her things, in case she changed her mind and was sorry and came home.

Peculiar stuff. Drawings of women who were half animals, dismembered bodies, coloured shapes that meant nothing, the kind of paintings children do. With the notebooks, the same. A jumble of words and scribble and doodles. Modern poetry, some of it looked like, no rhyme or anything, hard to make out what she was trying to say, bits and pieces of stories, bits about sex, just showing off she knew the words, bits about dreams. Mostly nonsense. If I try to remember any of it, sounds silly, like this:

FREDERICA

(this is an elegy for the mother I remember, whose breast my tiny hands patted as I searched for her with my mouth wanting her so much drawing her into me. She talked to me in a secret language of mamabébé. She was my place once and I was hers. I didn't give her up without a struggle)

My mother was my first great love, she was my paradise garden, and she was the Queen of Heaven, she was not that soppy lady Mary but someone far more beautiful and fierce, she was lion-soft and flushed and sexy, she smelled of herself, of her own body, she shouted out, she was powerful. She was a goddess who went disguised in the suburbs, but I recognized her, in my eyes nothing could diminish her grandeur.

(an elegy for the mother I lost, when the skin that bound us ripped away, our separate skins tore off and we were miserable being two being so different she couldn't like me being so unlike herself and this is also an elegy for the mother I found again she thought I had abandoned her and given her

173

up for ever but I had not I needed to go away so that I could come back just as she did)

Who can remember being born? Martin says he can remember being carried in his father's arms, his father pacing to and fro in the tiny kitchen at the back of the ground-floor flat and patting him with big hands to comfort his crying. I can remember staring from my pram at the grey sky, I remember the wooden bars of the play pen through which I gazed, and the red bars of the electric fire which frightened me, they were so angry.

(this is a love song for my daughter not yet born, who swims inside me dreaming unborn dreams, my flesh and blood, made of love in the land of milk and honey, the land of spices and stories)

When I left home, when I ran down Holloway Road to the tube with the mother's words EVIL and MAD in my ears and my father's words YOU LITTLE SLUT YOU LITTLE WHORE I ran very fast, to escape their words, I put on a disguise so that someone else could feel the bite and sting of those words but not me. I changed into someone else and escaped. My flesh was branded with those words for everyone to see, I had to cover myself with a man's clothes then run.

(a love song for my daughter who is nearly ready to be born rippling through my silk insides down my pink silk slide)

I left home a second time. Madame Lesley sold me the pink chiffon frock so that I could come out in style. I was sick with fear of the unknown world outside my parents' house, the path to the gate dissolved under my feet, only pride kept me from crying, I walked on the red and black tiles past the silvery dustbins through the scent of wallflowers out to the road where Martin waited for me in the van. I had a new skin to try on. I pulled it round me, a skin of pictures and words.

(a prayer for my daughter that I will not harm her and that Martin will not, that we will not burden or bruise her too much, that she will know how she is longed for and waited for flesh of my flesh)

In the coffee-bar after watching *Pierrot le Fou*, I told Martin about the blood, that it was six weeks late, that I was going to have a baby. He closed his eyes then opened them, turquoise blue and translucent. In between our joined mouths was cappuccino froth, the taste of milky lather, sprinkled chocolate and coffee.

(a prayer for my daughter that I shall be able to contain her while she grows, inside and outside me, that I shall be able to see her through while she needs me then let go, not to bind or fetter her but to see her as she is, different the same, to love her with imagination and plenty)

We will both paint, Martin and I said to each other: and we will both mind the baby. We were young, and full of hope. It was the sixties. So we walked back through Soho and into the next story: